The Desert Rats

The Mason Braithwaite Paranormal
Mystery Series, book 2

Also in this series:

Signs Point to Yes

The Desert Rats

Reach for the Sky

Billy Blood

Rubber-Band Ball

The Invisible Arrow

Penstock Canyon

The Man from Grapalia

The Mythical Blond

Stealth Glasses

The Melted Pineapple

Night on the Water

The Landers Mystique

The Desert Rats

Published by Dagmar Miura
Los Angeles
www.dagmarmiura.com

The Desert Rats

This is a work of fiction. Names, characters, businesses, places, events, and incidents are either the products of the author's imagination or used in a fictitious manner. Any resemblance to actual persons, living or dead, or actual events is purely coincidental.

First published 2015

ISBN: 978-1-942267-07-2

The
Desert
Rats

Christopher Church

THE STRANGENESS HAD STARTED when they were driving up the last stretch of desert back road to Daniel's place on Friday—and Mason, in the passenger seat, was the only one who noticed it. Out of nowhere, a set of headlights appeared in front of them. Ned dimmed his lights, and so did the other vehicle. Mason looked at the car as it went by. It was a Crown Vic, the same vintage as Ned's, he realized. Weirdly, the driver looked a lot like Ned—the same Latin coloring, straight black hair in the same natty style. His heart started to pound.

"That was us," Mason said. It wasn't someone who looked like Ned, he realized, it *was* Ned. And that was Peggy in the backseat. They had just driven past themselves.

Thursday

"Why Albuquerque?" Mason asked, rubbing sleep out of his eyes. He had just padded down the hall from their bedroom and was trying to get the espresso machine working. Ned had been up for hours, which was logical, as it was nearly eleven, and the sun blazed through the French doors.

"There's a festival there this week, hot-air balloons. Dozens of them. What's more fun than balloons?" He came over and took the filter handle from Mason's fumbling hands. "Let me do it," he said, and kissed Mason before nudging him away. Mason sat at the open counter that divided their kitchen from the living room. To Mason, pre-coffee, it seemed like Ned was moving in fast-forward.

"But isn't it kind of far to go for a mini vacation? You said you wanted to drive, but I thought you meant somewhere close, like Palm Springs."

"It's about twelve hours' drive from LA, so we could do it in two days, and maybe stay in Flagstaff, check out the Grand Canyon before the winter."

"Or we could fly?"

"But half the fun is in the road trip," Ned said, deftly snapping the filter handle into the espresso machine.

"OK," Mason said. "I know you like driving. Maybe it won't be as hot as I think it's going to be."

"It's high desert most of the way out there, so it won't be hot at all."

Mason thought that sounded more like spin than fact. "How much time can you take away from your work?"

"A few days will be fine. I'll take my computer and do stuff out there if anything urgent comes up." Ned worked with bankers on something to do with mortgages, which didn't sound to Mason like it should ever involve any urgency; since he worked from home, it made sense that he could spoof a regular work day while he was on the road.

"What about you?" Ned asked. "Can the psychic world exist without your input for a couple of days?"

"If my psychic cash flow hadn't already been established, I wouldn't even consider a vacation."

Just a few weeks earlier Mason had been thrown out of his office job, and rather than hunting for another one, he had decided to try to make a living as a psychic investigator. By honing his psychic skills, along with some old-school research, he'd started earning an income almost right away. Ned had resisted the change at first, and he was still skeptical about whether Mason's work involved truly psychic inspiration, but once there was money coming in he had calmed down about it.

"Besides," Mason said, "I can use my extrasensory connections no matter where I am."

"I don't suppose there'll be a huge demand for your services once you're out of this crazy city." Ned poured the entire pot of espresso into a big cup and handed it to him.

"I'd argue that, if you hadn't just made my coffee," Mason said. "But either way I have no intention of looking for work while we're away. It'll be a couples thing, just you and me and the balloons."

"About that," Ned began, but he stopped when their roommate, Peggy, walked in.

"Have you told him?" she asked.

"Told me what?" Mason said, color rising in his face. As a redhead his emotional states were often quickly obvious on his pale skin; he thought that was probably why redheads were stereotyped as hotheaded. He realized Peggy looked like she'd been up for hours already too. Morning people, how do they do it, he wondered. "Hey, wait a minute—isn't it a work day?" he asked her. Peggy worked for lawyers, who kept religiously to the nine-to-six Monday-to-Friday schedule.

"It is, but I broke up with Van last night, so I'm taking some mental health time, starting today."

"Oh, I'm sorry to hear that," Mason said.

"Don't be," she said. "It was inevitable, and I'll be a lot better off. But I need some time to recover. And, I've been doing a lot of evening gigs but neglecting my songwriting. So I'm going to spend a week or two writing some music. It's time for Peggy Pregnant to drop an album."

"Great idea," Mason said. Her stage persona, Peggy Pregnant, performed what Ned called "depression music," but Mason would more charitably label dark folk music. Her shtick was that Peggy Pregnant was enormously pregnant, wearing a fake belly under her 1960s flower-child garb as she strummed her acoustic guitar. Peggy Pregnant had being playing venues around town for years, and no one ever asked why she hadn't had the baby yet.

"Maybe New Mexico will inspire me," she said. "It's always easier to focus on writing when you're not in your own house."

The espresso was finally kicking in. "You're coming with us," Mason said, forcing a pleasant smile.

"I was about to ask you about that," Ned said.

"Is that OK?" Peggy said.

"It's fine with me," Mason said. "It'll be fun to do a road trip, just the three of us." It would be fun to have Peggy along, but he was a little thrown by the fact that they'd discussed it without him. The things you miss when you don't get up early. "When are we leaving?" he asked.

"I figure mid-afternoon tomorrow," Ned said. "There'll be traffic, but we can use the carpool lane."

Mason cut up some fruit for his breakfast and walked down the hall to the office he and Ned shared. Their house was on a hillside, and the bedrooms and the living room, facing downhill, had sun all day, but the office was on the uphill side, facing the street: a dark little yin enclave where it was easy to focus on work. He opened his computer and started an email to Miss Cassie, his shrink. They had a standing appointment on Fridays.

> Dear Miss Cassie,
> Ned and I are going out of town this week-
> end, and we'll be leaving around the time my
> appointment is scheduled with you tomorrow.
> I'm so sorry I have to cancel, but I'll see you next
> week.
> Mason

Mason didn't really think he needed psycho-therapy, but he had done some psychic investiga-tion work for Miss Cassie, and she had essentially manipulated him into becoming her client. She was skeptical of his psychic abilities and assumed he had used more prosaic means to find answers. But at the same time, she was clearly intrigued, as they talked a lot about his psychic experiences in their head-shrinking sessions.

He wanted to spend some time today working on his business, maybe listing his name on some local psychic websites or even buying some ad space. But before he had time to start on that, an email popped up.

> Hi Mason,
> No problem. Let's meet at 10 tomorrow; that'll give you plenty of time to get ready for your trip.
> Cassie

Mason groaned. He obviously wasn't going to get off so easily. He could cancel, he knew, but sometimes he got something out of his sessions with Miss Cassie. He hated talking about his life, and it was hard work answering her questions, but she had a knack for getting him thinking about what he was doing, how he was dealing with his new career. The truly hard part was going to be getting up that early. A moment later another email popped up, this one from Miss Cassie's calendar, reminding him of his appointment the next morning. *I guess that's that,* he thought.

He spent the afternoon on his computer, reading about how to promote himself, connecting with someone who might build a website for him, submitting a listing on a local blog. Now and then he heard the sound of Peggy's guitar from her room, and her voice softly trying out lyrics. Ned came in and out of the office as his workday progressed, sometimes sitting at his computer, sometimes getting up to take a phone call on the balcony outside the French doors. Mason really loved this kind of day, still fairly new to him. At first he had felt guilty at not having a routine or a place to go every morning, but with Ned's encouragement he got used to setting his own schedule. He'd been worried that he and Ned might start to clash, being home together all day, but so far it had been fine.

After dinner, Mason pulled his duffel bag out of the bedroom closet. "What's the weather going to be like?" he asked Ned, who was lying on the bed reading.

"You're the psychic; ask your spirit guides."

"I'm not that kind of psychic. My power derives directly from the untapped dimensions of reality," he said firmly. Rather than engaging Ned's skepticism by debating with him, he had started reinforcing his version of reality by presenting it as fact, not something open to debate. He had enough doubts in his abilities himself; taking Ned's disbelief on board would be overwhelming. He had to work to stay positive about his new line of work, and remind himself that even though he didn't really understand the mechanism, he'd had some important insights when he needed them.

"Well, ask Google, then," Ned said, looking

up at him. And then, incredulous, "Are you wearing a ring?"

"Oh, yeah. I found it in a drawer." He held out his right hand for Ned's closer inspection. It was a simple silver band that he'd forgotten about.

"Are you trying to tell me something?"

"Dude, it's not about you," he said, pulling his hand away. "I bought it when I was backpacking in Southeast Asia, before my descent into a life of corporate drudgery. Now it kind of reminds me of that time."

AFTER THEY'D SETTLED INTO bed and Ned had fallen asleep, Mason gave himself the suggestion that he'd have a lucid dream, an important tool in his psychic arsenal. If he could become aware that he was in the dream world, he could manipulate the dream and hopefully gain insight into the waking world. He wasn't sure if he was getting any better at it. He'd often get vivid but unexplained images in the hypnagogic state, between drowsiness and sleep, but once he was dreaming he found it difficult to take charge of the dream. Even when he did, he wasn't convinced he was accomplishing anything.

That night, he did realize he was dreaming at one point, and to prevent the dream from evaporating, as happened so often when he tried to change it, he decided just to experience it as an observer. He was drifting in a field of static. It felt like floating in a swimming pool, but all around him was the snowy garble and white noise of an old TV tuned to a dead channel. Suddenly everything seemed to drop downward—he was still floating, but felt supported now. The static cleared and his surroundings settled into darkness and silence. The darkness wasn't indifferent nothingness; it was something present and tangible. He wasn't sure what it meant, but as the sensation gradually faded, he willed himself to wake up. He pulled his notepad out of the drawer in the nightstand and scribbled what he could remember of the feeling of the dream. In this business, he'd learned, it was important to keep track of everything, as the significance might not be clear until later.

Friday

"OH, MY GOD, NO," Mason said when his alarm went off. It was eight o'clock, and he could hear Ned in the kitchen. He blinked a few times so as not to fall asleep again, and rolled out of bed.

"How do you people function at this hour?" he asked Ned when he'd made it down the hall.

"I've been up for a while, boyfriend," he said. "I knew you'd be getting up, so I made coffee."

Mason drank the first pot of espresso and started on another, munching on some muesli and fruit. By nine o'clock he was awake enough to get dressed, pull on his backpack, and head outside into the bright sunshine. He pulled his bicycle out of the garage and coasted down the hill to the boulevard. Miss Cassie's office was downtown, right across the street from the metro, so he locked up his bike at the station in his neighborhood rather than taking it with him.

He loved coming up out of the ground to Miss Cassie's building; it was a 1930s art deco gem that made his heart soar just walking into it. It almost made the head-shrinking seem like an excuse to come down here. The building's facade and the lobby, even the elevator doors, were preserved from the building's youth, but riding up to Miss Cassie's office was like time-traveling to the twenty-first century. Her spare, industrial office space had plain concrete floors and very little furniture apart from her desk, a sofa, and easy chairs. Even her bookcases were dwarfed by the twelve-foot ceilings.

He glanced at his phone as he got off the elevator. He was ten minutes early. The sliding sign on Miss Cassie's office door said "Come in," so he pulled it open anyway.

"Mason," she said, looking up from her desk. "Always a pleasure. I'm glad you were able to reschedule. Have a seat. I'll just be a minute."

He hadn't had much choice about rescheduling, he thought, but didn't say anything, and took his usual spot on the sofa, setting his backpack on the floor between his feet. He still felt a little groggy and wished he'd used his early arrival time to buy a coffee. Miss Cassie's tall windows looked out on the office towers of the financial district. It really was glammy, he thought, and he always felt content in her yang space, so different from his own comfortable little yin office at home.

Finally she walked around her desk and sat across from Mason, holding her tablet and a stylus. Miss Cassie was in her fifties, Mason guessed, and had a little weight on her frame, but always wore tailored suits that deemphasized it. Today it was a dark skirt and blazer with an expensive-looking scarf. He felt comfortable with her, maybe even some sense of kinship, as the work he'd done for her before he became her client had involved digging into her personal life, and he knew some of her secrets. But these days she was ever the professional.

"Last time," she began, "we were talking about control."

"I've been thinking about that. I was wondering if you think I'm a control freak. Because I don't really think I'm controlling."

"We were actually talking about your psychic work. My question is whether you use your psychic sense, as you say, because it's something that's only yours. Other people can't really challenge you on what you intuit psychically, so you're completely in charge of it."

"I don't think it's only me. I think anyone can access the information, like I do, through lucid dreams."

"The kind of dream that you can control," she said, looking to her tablet and scratching notes on it.

"Well, yes," Mason said tentatively.

"So, then, how engaged are you with the real world? Is it possible that you feel powerless in your real life, and these lucid dreams are a substitute for engaging with more tangible things?"

"I think I'm doing all right in the real world," he said, feeling his face reddening. "I'm making a living—you know that."

"But are you in charge of your life in the real world?"

"Hell, yes," he said, too loudly. He took a deep breath. "I quit my crappy job and invented another one. That makes me feel like I'm in charge of my life. And the lucid dreaming isn't a replacement for reality—it's just for getting information beyond the real world."

"The dreams feel real?"

"Yes, although things happen that make them seem unreal too. But they're very vivid."

"How do you know you're not lucid dreaming right now?" she asked.

"Good question," he said, and smiled. He thought for a moment. "When I'm in a lucid dream, I'm aware that I'm dreaming. Right now, I don't have that feeling; ergo, I'm not dreaming."

"You're aware of it every time? Sometimes when I have a nightmare, I'm sure it's real until I wake up."

"That's the lucid part," Mason said emphatically. "I'm aware it's a dream, and I can force myself to wake up."

"I knew you'd say something like that," Ned said, irritated. "That's why I didn't want to tell you. I think you have gender issues."

"Ned, I'm just kidding."

"But me getting a manicure makes you uncomfortable, right? It's like it threatens your masculinity."

"No, it doesn't, but the idea is pretty funny. And why have you been keeping it a secret? I've always thought you were just effortlessly well-kept, but clearly there's more to it."

"It's not a secret," Ned said defensively.

"But you are getting upset about it. Maybe you're the one with gender issues. You grew up with all those macho boys."

"Mason," he said, exasperated, "leave my family out of it. I'm going to get my nails done, which isn't emasculating, and it isn't a secret."

"Fair enough. Can I come? I've never done that. Does it hurt? Is it expensive? Where are you going to get it done?"

"It doesn't hurt," he said, laughing now. "Pretty Nail Blowout on Sunset."

"Let's roll," Mason said. "I'll be happy if my nails turn out even half as pretty as yours."

"My god, Mason, you are a handful." He shook his head. "Should we take the Barracuda or the Crown Vic?"

"I think the only thing that makes sense for a nail run would be the Barracuda," he said.

Ned was an auto fanatic, and the Barracuda

was a vintage muscle car that he kept in pristine condition. He navigated it deftly down the narrow, hilly streets of their neighborhood and onto the boulevard, heading west toward Hollywood. Mason insisted on a pit stop at a coffeehouse so he could get a triple espresso. Soon after, they pulled into a strip mall parking lot.

"Of course it's in a strip mall," Mason said, climbing out of the car.

"You were expecting something flashier? Cheap rent means they can charge reasonable prices."

"So you've been here before. Do you do this regularly?"

"Maybe once or twice," he said vaguely.

When they stepped inside, Mason saw that there were a couple of women having their nails worked on in the back, but no other guys. A petite woman seated at the front desk greeted them, a broad smile on her face. "Mr. Ned, welcome! The usual for you? Miss Diu isn't in today, but the new boss can take care of you, Miss Hanh. You brought a friend?"

"What's the usual?" Mason asked, looking from her to Ned.

"Very simple man's manicure," she said. "No color, no polish, very handsome."

"How am I just learning this about you?" Mason said. "Mister Pretty Nails."

Ned ignored him and spoke to the clerk. "I'll have the usual, and my boyfriend here wants a full set of French tips."

"That doesn't sound right," Mason said dubiously. "I don't think I want that."

The clerk giggled and said, "We'll set you up with a plain manicure too. I'm sure you'll love it."

She led Mason to a work station with a demure young woman who took hold of his hands and looked at them with concern. Ned sat at another station and waited for Hanh. Mason's manicurist gently pulled his ring off his right hand, then tapped his left ring finger and nodded toward Ned. "No marry?"

"No." Mason grinned and shook his head.

A door in the back swung open and Hanh appeared, eyeing Mason, then sitting with Ned and briefly introducing herself to them both. She had a dramatic haircut, Mason noticed, longer in front than in back, coming to two sharp points below her chin.

Ned chatted with her as she set to work, but Mason's manicurist didn't speak much English, so he sat in silence while she chatted in Vietnamese with the other staffers. At one point they all laughed; the focus seemed to be on Mason.

"What's so funny?" he asked Ned.

Hanh looked up at him and said in flawless English, "They think your red hair is funny. Not funny ha-ha, just funny unfamiliar."

"Well, they're laughing like it's funny ha-ha," Mason said. He could feel his face getting red, and realized that would probably induce even more hilarity.

"They're not doing it to be mean," Ned said.

"You speak Vietnamese now?" Mason asked him, raising his eyebrows.

Hanh looked up from Ned's nails again. "In Asia they'd think you were a river goblin, because goblins are tall like you and have red hair."

"Of course they do," Mason said.

Ned ignored him and said to Hanh, "You sound like you grew up here."

"Mostly," she said, and smiled to herself as she worked on his hands.

Mason's manicurist said something in Vietnamese, and Hanh translated. "She wants to know if she can touch your eyebrows," she said.

"Absolutely not," Mason said sharply. The young woman must have understood that, as she smiled gently and looked back to her work.

"How is it that I'm a freak in my own city?"

"You're not a freak," Ned said. "And it's not your city; it's all of ours. They're just not used to seeing the red hair."

"They're all flirting with you, and it's like I'm some damn Sasquatch." He was often mystified at the effortless way Ned moved through the world. Ned was Latino, and of average height, so he fit in easily wherever he was; but he also had a way of presenting himself that Mason could never emulate. He looked more polished when he rolled out of bed than Mason could after four hours of highly focused grooming.

"I wasn't flirting with your boyfriend," Hanh

said. "Just for the record."

When they had paid and walked out to the car, Mason took a good look at his fingers in the daylight. "Not bad," he said. "I can't believe I didn't know that guys were allowed to get their nails done. Or that you did it on a regular basis."

"You don't know everything about me," Ned said.

"I guess I don't. This certainly gave me a glimpse behind the curtain."

"Where were you two?" Peggy asked when they walked into the house. She had a camping cooler perched up on the bar and was filling it with food from the refrigerator.

"We got manicures," Ned said.

"Pretty Nail Blowout?" she asked.

"How come I'm the only one who doesn't know about Pretty Nail Blowout?" Mason said.

"It's a good salon," Peggy said, and shrugged. "Let's see." They both held up their hands, and she said, "Ooh … pretty."

"What's the cooler for?" Mason asked.

"Once we leave town, there won't be anything vegan for you two to eat," she said. "So we're taking it with us."

"That's really thoughtful, thank you," Ned said. Peggy wasn't vegan herself, but she kept the house vegan out of respect for her roommates, and over the years she and Ned had become accomplished vegan cooks. Mason kept his own time in the kitchen to a minimum, but he ate well anyway thanks to them.

An hour later they had loaded their bags, Peggy's guitar case, and the cooler into Ned's other car, the Crown Vic. It was an enormous vehicle by modern standards, but a good size for a road trip. Mason offered to sit in the back, but Peggy refused. "You're way too tall for that," she said. "Rugby-size guys ride up front."

When they got down the hill to the freeway ramp and Ned skillfully nosed into the traffic, Peggy leaned in from the backseat and said, "We're actually doing this."

"It feels good, right, getting out of town," Ned said.

"It feels freaking amazing," she said. "Can I chip in for gas at some point?"

"We can figure that out afterward," Ned said. "This car gets about twelve miles to the gallon, so it's going to be a bit expensive. I should probably just cover it, because we did have cheaper options that I overruled."

"We wouldn't have all fit in my Prius, if that's what you mean," she said. "I'd like to chip in. If it gets too expensive maybe I can pawn some jewelry or something."

They rolled north out of the LA Basin and up through the Cajon Pass. The sky over the mountains took on the deep orange-pink of the Southwestern twilight.

"It's so beautiful here. The air is so clear," Mason said.

Somewhere in Ned's pants, his phone rang.

"No work today," Mason said. "Don't answer it."

Ned ignored him, and pressed his earpiece to pick up the call. Mason could only hear Ned's side of it, but he knew it wasn't good news.

"Oh, Gilbert, I'm so sorry…. When?" Ned listened, occasionally muttering "uh-huh."

"Uh-oh," Peggy said softly for Mason's benefit.

"Yeah, I can come up…. He's actually with me, we were driving out to New Mexico this weekend…. Really?… I guess you can ask him. We've got Peggy with us too; is it OK if we bring her?"

"Who died?" Peggy asked when Ned had ended the call.

"Gilbert's dad," he said. "Yesterday, out here in the desert, in Lancaster. He lives out here. It wasn't unexpected, but they thought he had a few more months. Cancer."

"Aw, hell," Peggy said. She had lost her mother to the disease a few years before. "Did you know him very well?"

"Not recently. I knew him when we were growing up. He wasn't an easy guy, but he and Gilbert were close."

"So you're going out there?" Mason asked.

"I'm sorry to blow up the road trip, but yes, I want to be with Gilbert right now." He slowed down and took the next exit off the highway.

"OK," Mason said. "That makes sense. He's an old friend. Maybe you can drop Peggy and me at a Metrolink station on the way. It'll save you a trip all the way back into town." It wasn't optimal, but he pushed his disappointment aside to be supportive of Ned.

"Gilbert asked if you could come too."

"Really? Why?" Gilbert was Ned's friend, and Mason accepted him for that reason, but he made Mason nervous. It always seemed like he was up to something, and even though he was apparently straight, he flirted shamelessly with men and women alike. He was also a sucker for a conspiracy story, which made Mason think he was gullible and maybe not too bright. But then, Ned thought Mason's worldview was similarly unrealistic.

"He said you might be able to help him. I'm assuming it's psychic power work."

"If he wants me to communicate with his dead father, no way. I'm not that kind of psychic."

"I have no idea what it is, but if that's the case, you can tell him that yourself. Are you up for coming with me?"

"As long as there's a bedroom for us," Mason said. "I don't think I'd sleep very well in the same room as Gilbert."

"Peggy, I'm sorry to ruin your trip too. Do you want to come with us, or do you want me to run you back to the city first?"

"His dad has a ranch out there, right? Will his mother be there?"

Ned had pulled into a deserted gas station parking lot, and he turned around to talk to Peggy. "His mother's gone too, years ago. And it's really just a house with a couple of horses in a corral, but it's a decent size, three or four bedrooms. I'm sure you'd have space to write. It's definitely in the countryside. The nearest neighbor's house is just a dot in the distance across the sand."

"Well, my plan was to get out of town and write some songs. So yeah, I'll come with you, if it's cool with him."

"He'll be glad to have the company." Ned pulled his phone out of his pants. "I have no idea how to get there from here, but I think we're kind of on the way. I always have to get there by GPS." He tapped and swiped on his phone. "Here we go; Rancho Daniel." He pronounced it the Spanish way, *dañel*. "The map just says 'rural road, Natron, California.' But it's only an hour and a half's drive from here."

"Natron? Seriously?" Peggy said, leaning toward them. "I thought you said Lancaster. Is it the Natron that's in the Mojave?"

"Yeah," Ned said, twisting around again. "Daniel's place isn't really near Lancaster; that's just where the hospital is. His house is at Natron, and it's definitely in the middle of the Mojave."

"That's so bizarre," she said. "You know I've been emailing with my half-brother—he has a cabin in Natron. He goes up there on weekends in the winter."

"Are you sure it's Natron?" Ned said. "I've been there, and there's no town or anything. It's just a crossroads. It was something like a silver mining camp a hundred years ago, but now it's just desert."

"That's the place," she said. "I'm sure of it. Can you believe that? What are the odds?"

"There are no coincidences," Mason said. "There's something deeper going on."

Ned said, "Not the psychic power, Mason, please. Not now."

"Think about it, man," Mason said, annoyed at being censored, especially when he'd been so patient with the abrupt change of plans. "How can this be a coincidence?" As he tried to sharpen his psychic insights, Mason had come to understand that there were connections running through the world that weren't immediately apparent. If Ned couldn't even contemplate the idea, he was missing something, like someone walking around at night and never looking up at the stars. If Peggy and Ned both had a connection to a crossroads in the Mojave Desert, it had to be meaningful.

"What else could it be?" Peggy asked.

"Synchronicity," Mason said. "Hidden connections running through the universe."

Ned rubbed his eyes and sighed.

The gas station attendant stuck his head out the door of the shop. Even though it was evening and summer was over, it was still warm enough that he was wearing a short-sleeved shirt. He looked concerned, Mason thought—probably because the only vehicle in his parking lot was just sitting there idling. People sometimes mistook the Crown Vic for an unmarked cop car, but a quick look at its occupants would dispel that notion. Ned waved, and the attendant nodded and went back inside.

Ned turned and looked back to Peggy. "Do you think your brother will be up there this weekend?"

"I'm sure he won't. It's still too hot."

"Well, then it's not something we need to worry about now," Ned said, and shifted the car into drive. Mason knew better than to say any more, but he looked back at Peggy, and they shared a glance. They both knew Ned well enough to see he was upset, even if he had shifted into coping mode.

Ned navigated away from the freeway and onto a two-lane highway heading north across the desert. "Have you met the guy yet?" he asked Peggy.

"No, I haven't even talked to him on the phone. But we've been emailing. At first he didn't even believe my story, but he's warming up." With Mason's help, Peggy had recently learned of her half-brother's existence. "I'm kind of freaked out about it too. You know: Will he look like me? Will we have the same mannerisms? What if he's an ass or a sociopath or something?"

"I have a bunch of brothers," Ned said, "and

they do look like me, and some of them can be asses, but it's not scary."

"But you've always known them. I've never met this guy. It's daunting."

"I wouldn't put it off too long," Ned said. "Like Daniel used to say, 'It's later than you think.'"

NED FOLLOWED HIS PHONE'S directions across the desert as night fell, zigzagging through the countryside on rural highways. They stopped at a supermarket in the last little town before Daniel's place; Ned was sure that food would be the last thing on Gilbert's mind right now, so they bought enough supplies to last a few days.

"We ain't in Kansas anymore," Mason said as they walked back out to the car.

"What do you mean?" Ned asked him.

"The people in there. They're all rugged and surly."

Peggy said, "I noticed that too. Leathery skin, zero grooming, and everyone dressed like it's rodeo weekend."

"They're called desert rats," Ned said. "That's the way everyone is out here. It's kind of refreshing, isn't it, after living in a city that's obsessed with haircuts and bust size? Daniel kind of became a desert rat too after he moved out here full-time."

"They should at least moisturize. The sun out here must be brutal," Peggy said.

Mason said, "It's off-putting for me, the gruffness."

"It's just because they like the solitude," Ned said. "If it makes you feel any better, they're not any more dangerous than city folk."

Back on the highway, Ned slowed the car to a crawl when the map on his phone showed that the last turn was imminent. "Daniel's road should be right here," he said, turning on his brights. Finally it appeared in the headlights, little more than a rutted dirt track.

"It's just about a mile in from this corner," Ned said, gingerly pulling onto the road. The first section had a washboard surface that rattled the car, and Ned crawled along, but soon it smoothed out and he was able to pick up some speed.

And then, seemingly out of nowhere, a set of headlights appeared in front of them. Ned turned off his brights just as the other car did the same. "Gilbert must have had other visitors today," he said.

Ned hugged the right shoulder, but the road was wide enough that he didn't have to slow down much to pass. Mason looked at the car as it went by. It was a Crown Vic, the same vintage as Ned's, he realized, and the same color. Weirdly, the driver looked a lot like Ned, and in the backseat he caught a glimpse of someone's head, leaning against the side window, with long brown hair. His heart started to pound.

"That was us," he said. It wasn't someone who looked like Ned, he realized, it *was* Ned. And Peggy in the back.

"What was me?" Ned said absently. Obviously he hadn't seen it.

"Did you look at that car? Peggy, did you see that?" he said.

"No," she said.

Ned said, "I just saw the glare of the head-lights. I was watching the road. Was it Gilbert? He said he'd be there tonight."

"No, it was us," Mason said, adamant. "It was the Crown Vic, and you were driving, and Peggy was in the back."

"Not possible, boyfriend, because we're right here. How could we be in two places at once?"

"Was it maybe a psychic flash?" Peggy asked. "Because, like the man said, we're right here."

"Well, obviously," Mason said, "but I know what I saw." This was way beyond any debate about coincidences and synchronicities, he thought; this was downright weird. And how could they be so disinterested? His heart was pounding.

"Strange things do happen up at Daniel's place," Ned said dreamily, looking straight ahead.

"What is wrong with you two?" Mason said, looking from one to the other. "I just had a majorly freaky experience. We just passed us: three people who look just like us, in this exact car. This, like, blows the lid off reality as we know it."

"Does it?" Peggy said softly. Mason twisted around to scowl at her, but she was staring out the window. "It's really dark here," she said. "The stars almost reach down to the horizon."

"Oh, my god," Mason said, and folded his arms. They were both completely in denial. That was to be expected from Ned, but Peggy was usually at least open to listening to him. Was he supposed to keep his surreal experiences to himself now? They rode on in silence. He looked at Ned again. He was staring straight ahead, hands languorous on the steering wheel. He looked back at Peggy, who still stared out the window, motionless. Maybe it was more than just disinterest, Mason thought. Maybe they just couldn't handle such intense strangeness, so they tuned it out, some part of their minds protecting them from it. His resentment started to evaporate. Maybe I really am on this journey alone, he thought.

"We're here," Ned said, coming back to life. In the headlights Mason could see a corral, a battered pickup truck, and Gilbert's familiar sedan in front of the house. The outside light was on, and as they pulled up Gilbert came out to greet them. Ned gave him a long hug.

"Edgar! Thank you for coming," Gilbert said, using the unabbreviated and unanglicized version of Ned's name. "You're all here. It's so good to see you."

"I'm so sorry about your dad," Peggy said, giving him a hug.

"Thank you, missy. He was a scrappy guy, but he lost this battle."

Mason embraced him as well, and felt Gilbert's

33

hand rest on his buttock for just a moment too long. Maybe it's because I'm taller, Mason reasoned, and that's just where his hand landed. Nonetheless, it was classic Gilbert, quickly managing to throw him off balance.

Gilbert helped them carry their bags and groceries into the house. It was a great place, Mason thought, rustic in design but with high ceilings, lots of broad windows, and best of all, airconditioning. It was huge, with multiple doorways leading off the main hallway. Gilbert put Peggy's guitar case in one of the smaller bedrooms, but showed Ned and Mason into the largest one.

"Are you sure you don't want the master?" Ned said. "It's your house now."

"That's my dad's room, *cabrón*. I'm not sleeping in there," he said.

Ned put his arm around Gilbert's shoulders. "Have you eaten today?"

"Does a microwave burrito count?" he asked.

"No, it doesn't. I'm going to make some real food." Ned set to work in the kitchen, and Gilbert sat with Peggy and Mason nearby at the kitchen table. He talked about the last few weeks with his father, the rapid decline, driving back and forth to the hospital every day. Peggy shared her parallel experiences of losing her mother.

"You're an orphan now, like me," she said finally.

Tears welled up in Gilbert's eyes. Mason was surprised; he'd never seen him reveal much beyond bluster. "Sorry," Gilbert said, and wiped at his eyes.

"You never have to apologize for that," Peggy said, and Gilbert put his head down on his arms.

Death shatters people, Mason thought. He'd never seen Gilbert so emotional, so red and raw.

Gilbert brightened a little when Ned set out a platter of quesadillas and a plate of sliced cucumbers. "Are these vegan?" he asked Ned, picking up a wedge of quesadilla and inspecting it.

"Yeah, it's vegan cheese, if you can believe that."

"How is that even possible?"

"Cheese isn't about cow's milk," Ned said. "It's about fermentation. It's usually made out of dairy products, but you can make it out of cashews or whatever."

Gilbert took a small bite, and must have deemed it edible, because he loaded up his plate and ate with gusto.

When they were finished, Mason said, "So, Gilbert, why did you want me to come up here with Ned?"

"Well," Gilbert said, leaning back in his chair, "I thought you could help me. My dad had some stuff that I want to know more about. I think it might be important. Maybe you could do some research for me? I'll pay you, of course."

Mason said, "Do you mean psychic research, like psychometry?"

"What's that?" Gilbert asked.

"It's when you hold an object in your hands and get psychic information from it. Keys, jewelry, that kind of thing."

"Oh, yeah, the reading thing. Maybe that, or maybe some library research. Whatever you could do that would actually work."

"OK, the psychic thing does work, just to put that out there," Mason said.

"Sweetie," Ned said, "he's not saying that he doubts you."

"It's a fine line, though, isn't it," Gilbert said, "between what you think you get from psychic insight and what you find out at the library, in the real world?"

Mason sighed. He didn't want to get annoyed with Gilbert, given his emotional state. He was literally in tears, his psyche a gaping wound. Mason had to make room for that, even though it felt like a personal attack.

"I guess it depends on what it is exactly that you want me to research."

"Can we get into that tomorrow?" Gilbert said. "It's been a long day."

"Sure," Mason said, and nodded. But he was curious about what Gilbert could possibly want him to do, if he was starting from a place of skepticism. At least it wasn't about communicating with the dead—that was work for a completely different kind of psychic.

"Let's go sit in the living room," Ned said, "and talk about something else."

Mason was glad for the change of subject; defending his work was becoming a grind.

"Can I open some wine? Ned, it won't bother you?" Gilbert asked.

"No, go ahead," he said. "In fact, let me do it. You go sit, and I'll bring it in."

Gilbert herded Peggy and Mason into the front room, plopping himself into a recliner. The house had clearly been set up as a second home, with basic, functional furniture and lots of pinewood. The front windows were massive, though, and Mason was startled by how dark it was outside.

"No curtains?" he asked Gilbert. "People could see in here for miles."

"There aren't any people out there to be looking in," Gilbert said.

"Was there someone here tonight, just before we arrived?" he asked Gilbert. Ned walked in just then, with three highball glasses and a bottle of wine, and looked at Mason, his brow furrowed. He didn't even remember the car passing them on the road, Mason realized. Not only had Ned tuned it out, he had erased it from his memory. Maybe I made it up, Mason thought, feeling a twinge of fear at doubting his own sanity. Miss Cassie would love that, him questioning his understanding of reality.

"Uh, no. I got back here around four, and you were the only visitors."

"You'll see in the morning," Ned said. "It's just miles of open space."

Peggy took a glass from Ned and held it up for him to pour. "Tell us about your dad," she asked Gilbert. "What kind of guy was he?"

"He was a great guy. He loved being out here, loved his horses," Gilbert said, taking a glass from Ned and stretching his feet out.

"He was a mean bastard when we were little, but I liked him more later on," Ned said.

"Isn't there some rule about not speaking ill of the dead?" Peggy said.

"Daniel doesn't care," Ned said, shrugging his shoulders. "He's dead."

"That's your nontheist understanding of it," Mason said, "but Gilbert might care."

Gilbert just shook his head. "I'm sure Ned's right. Although that's not what the priest said at the hospital. He gave my dad last rites and then gave me all this stuff to do to protect his immortal soul—planning a burial mass, a memorial mass, a vigil. I think he just wanted to keep me busy so I wouldn't focus on the grief."

"It's also a control mechanism to keep you following their rules," Ned said.

"I'm glad my dad's sisters are taking care of the funeral and all that in the city. That would have been overwhelming. They want me to stay out here and start to get things in order before I come back." He leaned forward and looked earnestly at Ned. "I'm so glad you came up here, Nedly. I'm sorry I trashed your getaway, but there's just so much stuff I need to figure out, and you're the guy. I've got so much to ask you about—stacks of paper three feet deep. Tomorrow, though, not now."

"I'm not worried about the trip, although I feel bad about dragging these two along."

"I'm happy to be here," Peggy said.

"And if we're going to be doing paperwork, my manicure won't be wasted," Ned said.

"How is Pretty Nail Blowout?" Gilbert asked. "I heard there's a new owner."

"Seriously?" Mason exploded. "How come I'm the only one who doesn't know about Pretty Nail Blowout?"

"It's one of our things," Ned said.

"So you both go there?"

"I think we started going there when we were getting ready for senior prom," Gilbert said.

"But why have I never heard of it?"

"It's not the kind of thing you need," Gilbert said simply.

"What's that supposed to mean? I don't need to have nice nails?" He wasn't able to suppress his frustration this time, even in the interest of protecting Gilbert.

"It's not that you've been excluded," Ned said. "It's just … uh … you have your own rugged sort of look. No manicure required."

"You make me sound like the desert rats in that supermarket," Mason said.

Ned said nothing, and Gilbert looked down at the carpet.

Mason looked sideways at Ned. "Sometimes I wonder if I really know you at all," he said.

"Jesus, Mason," Peggy said, "you're being a drama queen. It's not like he's out sleeping with someone else—he's just getting a manicure. You don't know everything about Ned, and he doesn't know everything about you. It's better that way, don't you think?"

"Yes, I suppose it is," he conceded, chastened. He knew that Peggy wouldn't be yelling at him if he weren't actually out of line. He forced himself to calm down and took a sip of his wine. "But I'm not a desert rat."

"Nobody said you were," Ned said.

"You're attractive when you get snippy," Gilbert said to Peggy. "It enhances your hotness."

There they were, Gilbert's true colors, Mason thought. Even in his distracted and fragile state of mind he was able to bring the lechery.

"Thank you," Peggy said, not missing a beat. "But I want to hear more about Daniel. What did he do for a living?"

"He ran a moving company. Just a couple trucks and five or six people on staff, but he did pretty well. We always had food on the table, and I was able to mooch off him well into adulthood." He smiled. "He started out as a roadie, actually, and that turned into moving furniture for people. He was a musician too. He played guitar, like you. He still messed around, recording himself, until recently. Did you see the music room?"

"No! Show me," she said, and jumped up.

Gilbert motioned for Ned and Mason to join them, and led them down the hall, past the bedrooms to the back of the house.

"It's huge," Mason said, stepping into the room. It was as large as the front room, with thick fabric mats padding the walls and ceiling. A couple of guitars perched on stands at one side, along with amps, pedals, and unidentifiable electronic equipment.

"Wow," Peggy said, looking around.

"Why are the walls padded?" Mason asked. "You said there aren't any neighbors."

"It's not to stop the sound from getting out—it's to stop the noise in the rest of the house from getting in," Gilbert said. "For recording. And it dampens the sound in the room so there's no echo."

"This is good-quality gear," Peggy said. "Can I use this stuff, maybe do some recording while we're here?"

"I'm sure he would have liked the idea of another musician taking advantage of this space. He put a lot of work into the soundproofing."

"I see that, but there's still a big window. Wasn't he worried about the noise?"

"There's no noise out there. We're in the middle of nowhere in the desert. He left the window because he loved the view of the landscape. He said it inspired him to write."

"I am so glad I brought my guitar," Peggy said.

They returned to the front room and chatted a while longer, finishing the bottle of wine. Finally Mason stood up and said, "Bedtime for me. See you in the morning, Gilbert. Can I ask, does your dad happen to have Wi-Fi?"

"Of course. This is the middle of nowhere, but we're not animals. The password is 'tesoro71.'" He spelled it out and added, "all lowercase."

Peggy said, "I'm going too. Good night, gents," and followed Mason back toward the bedrooms.

"Sorry that I yelled at you," she said before they parted, placing a hand on Mason's arm.

"I actually needed to hear that," Mason said, "so thank you. You're a lot more rational than I am sometimes."

"Not always, but I'm glad I can provide some perspective."

"You do. And I just need to accept that I'm not a Pretty Nail Blowout kind of guy."

"I'm glad you're not," she said.

Mason propped himself up in the bed and got his laptop online. He read his email and the news. An hour later Ned came in, collapsing onto the bed beside him.

"He seems to be doing pretty well," Mason said quietly, setting his laptop aside.

"I think he's OK, yeah. So you're not too bummed that we're not going to New Mexico?"

"Oh, hell, no. I wasn't attached to that at all. I'm glad you can be here with Gilbert. He really trusts you, you know."

"He always thought I was smarter than him, so he looks to me for help with book-smart stuff. But he's smart too, just in a different way."

"How's that?" Mason asked, unconvinced. Gilbert wasn't a dullard, but he wouldn't be winning any Nobel Prizes any time soon either.

"He's street-smart, I think, and people-smart. He could seduce anybody." He put his arm across Mason's waist and nuzzled his belly. "Not you, though. You wouldn't fall for it."

"I might, if he had a really good manicure."

Ned chuckled softly. "He always does."

DRIFTING OFF TO SLEEP, Mason told himself to dream about something significant. Eventually he became aware that he was floating, high above a lush green landscape. He was flying, gradually accelerating, the land below passing more quickly. It was exhilarating; he never dreamed about flying. Was that meaningful? He wondered how he would be able to land, and as soon as he did, he was on the ground. He was on a street in a city, with shops and signs. He couldn't read anything, even though it was in roman script; it was a foreign language, the letters dripping with accents. Vietnamese, he realized, and he willed himself awake, just long enough to groggily write on the notepad he'd left on the nightstand, "flying—landscape—important—Vietnamese."

Saturday

"I HATE TO DO THIS to you," Ned said, shaking Mason awake, "but I think you should get up."

"Aw, man, why? Is the house on fire?" Mason rolled over and rubbed his eyes.

"I made breakfast, and we're going to eat together outside, before it gets too hot out. You don't want to miss that. And I brought coffee for you."

"That's so sweet," Mason said. "Am I at least allowed to go pee first?" Ned laughed and left, and Mason sat up to find the cup, drinking as much of it as he could stomach. He could hear the others talking in the kitchen. He stumbled into his clothes and headed there.

Ned and Peggy were carrying plates out to the patio, where there was a big outdoor table and chairs that had been invisible last night in the darkness. Gilbert was already sitting out there. It was Mason's first look at the landscape, and it was remarkable.

"I see why your dad liked it here," he said, sitting down at the table. Flat scrubland stretched out to the horizon, broken only by a low mountain range at one side. Dry dormant bushes huddled here and there, waiting for the winter rains, and there were even a few spindly yuccas scattered around, though not nearly as many as in the national park farther south.

Ned had made a tofu scramble with colorful peppers, toast, and hash browns.

"This is delicious, man, even though it's not real food," Gilbert said.

"It'll feed your soul, not just fill your belly," Ned said. "And if you need 'real' food, you can have one of your microwaveable sodium burritos later."

"So why aren't there any neighbors?" Peggy asked. "It's really beautiful here, and your dad can't have owned all this land. I would think other people would want to live here too."

"His land ends about a hundred yards out there, but it abuts a big swath of public land. I'm not sure why it's public; maybe because there's an arroyo running through it. You can't really see the arroyo from here, but it's there, where the land is lowest. I've seen water run in it in winter when it's raining. If you look there, on the horizon, you can actually see a neighbor's house. It's miles away, so it's just a dot, but sometimes at night there's a light on there."

"You've also got someone camping on the public land," Mason said. In the middle of the plain was a silver glint beside a blotch of blue; it must have been a vehicle and a trailer.

"Oh yeah, I see it," Peggy said. "How did they get out there, though? There's no road that I can see."

"She has four-wheel drive," Gilbert said absently. "It's public land, so people camp. There's a hand pump with well water right there."

"But you said 'she.' You know who it is?" Ned asked.

"Her name's Laura. She camps out there sometimes. I've met her. She's quite shapely."

"Of course she is," Peggy said.

Ned ignored her and pressed Gilbert. "So how did you meet her? Did you walk over there or something?"

"I don't remember, man," he said angrily, not looking up from his food. "I just met her at some point, OK?"

"Dude, chill," Ned said, his eyes wide. "There's nothing to get upset about. I'm just asking you a question."

"Right," Gilbert said, and looked up, surprised now. "Sorry."

He had good reason to be on edge and over-ly sensitive, Mason thought, but Ned looked shocked.

"Strange things happen out there sometimes," Gilbert said.

"Ooh, Mason's specialty," Peggy said.

"What kind of strange things? Like this Laura woman?" Ned asked.

"My dad used to see weird things out there by the well. Once there were a set of headlights there in the night, just parked there, and then they went straight up in the sky and disappeared."

"So there was a UFO parked out there?" Ned said.

"Doesn't UFO just mean 'unidentified'?" Peggy asked.

Gilbert said, "These days it means a flying sau-cer—an alien spaceship."

He ought to know, Mason thought. A few months ago he'd had something removed from his forearm that he thought was an alien track-ing device. When it came to aliens, Gilbert was a wide-eyed believer.

"So was it a saucer?" Ned asked.

"Maybe," Gilbert said. "I didn't see it myself. But I've seen the blue lights. They just sort of wink on, float around, and wink off."

"Fireflies?" Peggy ventured.

"Fireflies don't live west of the Rockies. My dad thought the lights were more common in March, which does make it sound like an insect or something, but I've seen them at other times of the year too. And they're not little like a bug. They're big, and bright."

"How bizarre," Peggy said, pushing aside her empty plate and leaning in toward Gilbert.

He continued, "The Kawaiisu people—this was their land before the Spanish came—had stories about an ape-man kind of critter that lived around here. I'm glad I've never seen that."

"Wow," Mason said, mock-enthusiastically. "Aliens and bigfoot both. What more could you ask for?"

"Be nice," Ned said gently.

"You're all skeptical about aliens, but you claim to get messages from jewelry," Gilbert said.

"I've just never seen any real evidence," Mason replied, color rising to his cheeks. As much as he hated to admit it, Gilbert had a point.

"In my arm, man," Gilbert said, tapping his forearm and pointing to a small pink scar. "Don't you remember?"

Mason just nodded.

Peggy said, "I'm totally down with aliens. Maybe we'll see some of your blue lights if we sit out here tonight."

"Be careful what you wish for," Gilbert said.

"What do you mean?"

"People who see UFOs often have alien contact," Gilbert said. "This guy in Idaho blew that wide open recently when he published a bunch of his research on interviews with UFO witnesses.

When they go under hypnosis, they often find that they've had alien contact experiences that they didn't know about."

More of Gilbert's conspiracy theories, Mason thought, but he held his tongue. No way was he going to bring up the bizarre experience of passing their doppelgängers on the road the night before. He had decided it was some kind of psychic bleed-through meant just for him, since Peggy and Ned had completely tuned it out. But maybe there was more to it; maybe it was part of the strange phenomena around Daniel's place.

"Maybe that silver thing is a UFO parked out there right now," Peggy said. "Should we hike out there?"

"It's not a UFO, it's Laura," Gilbert said.

"Is there a pair of binoculars inside?" Ned asked.

"Yeah, good idea," Gilbert said, and got up to go into the house. When he came back he held the binoculars up to his eyes. "It's definitely Laura," he said, and passed them to Ned.

"Sweet classic Suburban," Ned said. "It must be about a 1970."

"Show me," Mason said after a minute, and Ned passed him the glasses. He cast around until he saw the silver glint, then focused in. The glare was from an Airstream trailer, and parked in front of it was a blue car, boxy and old. Nothing was visible but the trailer and the car, and there were no signs of life, just shimmering heat rising off the land.

Peggy took a look next. "I don't see your friend, but maybe we can hike out there later and say hello," she said.

"I wouldn't do that," Gilbert said, but didn't elaborate. "I'm going to clean up this stuff," he said, stacking their plates, "and then I'm going to put you to work, Mason."

"Great," Mason said.

AFTER HE'D LOADED THE dishwasher, Gilbert went into the back of the house, and a few moments later shouted for them to follow. They found him in another large room opposite the music room, this one laden with bookshelves lining the walls.

"My dad's library. It was another thing that he did, reading. He'd spend lots of time out here doing what he loved, especially after my mom died. That meant his horses, drinking bourbon, smoking cheroots, playing guitars, and reading. There wasn't a public library anywhere near here, so he'd buy boxes of used books to bring up with him." He pulled something off one of the bookshelves and tossed it at Mason. "Catch," he said.

Mason squealed, but managed to grab the thing as it struck his chest. It was heavy for its size, maybe four inches across. He looked at it and saw that it was a piece of jewelry, maybe a hairpin, but more likely a brooch, given the weight. It was gold and shaped in ornate spirals with delicate hammered flowers at the edges. "What is it?" he asked.

"That's what you're going to find out," Gilbert said.

"It was your dad's?"

"I think so. But it was hidden in a flowerpot. So my questions for you are, what the hell is it, where did it come from, and why was it hidden in my dad's stuff? It looks important, right?"

"It looks expensive," Ned said, taking it from Mason. "And if this is real gold, it's worth a fortune."

"I think it is gold," Gilbert said, "because it's soft. And it's not just plated. I scratched into it a little on the back."

Peggy took it and looked at it closely. "I think it's old, you guys. Doesn't it look handcrafted? It's still shiny, but gold doesn't tarnish, so it could be very old. There are these almost hook things on the back." She held it up against her shoulder. "It's a pin, don't you think? You'd wear it with an evening gown, on your chest."

"Can we see the pot it was in?" Mason asked.

"Out in the barn," Gilbert said. Peggy set the brooch carefully on a bookshelf, and the four of them went out the back door and trooped across the yard. The barn was more just a shed made of ancient weathered wood, with a similarly worn corral fence around the far end of it. Gilbert opened the broad door, which had a rudimentary latch but no lock, and they entered the dim interior. When his eyes adjusted to the light, Mason could see that some horse tack hung on one wall, but the horses were long gone. Near the door at the opposite end, leading out to the corral, were two stacks of terra-cotta pots. They were in garden sizes, eight to twelve inches across. Gilbert pushed the back door open so they could see better.

"Why would he have flowerpots up here anyway?" Ned asked.

"I know," Gilbert said. "You can't grow anything out here unless you're really focused on it, and he wasn't. I never saw him grow anything."

"You were smashing them up?" Peggy asked. Scattered over the hard-packed brown earth of the corral were bits of red rubble and dust, presumably from some of the pots.

Yeah," Gilbert said, sounding slightly embarrassed. "You know, you can't hang out at the hospital all day and all night, so I'd come back here for some downtime. I was poking around and saw these damn pots. They're not worth anything, and they're basically made out of dirt, right, so I was just returning them to the earth. It felt good, in a way, releasing some stress."

In the dim light Mason saw an aluminum baseball bat leaning against the wall. He picked it up and asked, "Your weapon of choice?"

"Yes. Do you want to try it?"

"I don't," Mason said, holding the bat with both hands and waggling it to feel its weight, "but I bet it feels great. What's coming back to me now is ninth-grade PE, trying to smash a hardball into next Tuesday."

Peggy said, "OK, if I may cut through the testosterone for a minute, which pot was the pin in?"

"Those," Gilbert said, and pointed to some shattered pieces on the ground that hadn't yet been pulverized. "But it wasn't just sitting in the bottom of the pot under some dirt—it was sealed into the thing. The only reason I found it is because I smashed it."

Peggy picked up one of the shards and took it outside into the sunlight. "This isn't terra-cotta like the others," she said. "Feel it."

"What is it?" Mason asked, propping the baseball bat against the wall and handling the shard.

"I think it's plaster of paris," she said. "Plant pots are made out of terra-cotta, because it weeps and breathes. All these others are terra-cotta. It doesn't make sense to use plaster of paris to make a plant pot."

"How do you know so much about this stuff?" Gilbert asked her.

"I was making it for a while, when I was learning to write cuneiform. Do you guys remember that?"

"Oh, yeah," Ned said quickly.

"Like it was yesterday," Mason said. Peggy was something of a Renaissance woman, and over the years she had undertaken learning a series of creative skills. They had both put on weight when she had been baking pies, got new winter socks when she learned to knit, and of course her knowledge of graphic design software had paid off when she had designed a logo for Mason's new business. But the messiest one had been the cuneiform. Peggy would mix up batches of plaster of paris in the kitchen and let it dry in flat slabs on the balcony; when it reached the consistency of damp clay, she would practice pressing a stylus into the plaster to make cuneiform script, the way Mesopotamian record-keepers had done millennia ago. It was messy, and they had both been happy when that passion had faded.

"You know," she said, "plaster of paris is usually white, which means that this has probably been dyed terra-cotta red."

"Damn, woman, you're good," Gilbert said.

"I'm going to have to split my fee with you," Mason said.

"But I'll let you tell them what this means," she said.

"I think it means that the brooch was hidden on purpose," Mason said slowly. "And the fact that it was with a bunch of other flowerpots means it was hidden in plain sight."

"I wonder if your dad did that," Ned said.

"You both said it was odd that he had flowerpots stored out here in the desert," Mason said. "So doesn't that imply that Daniel knew about the brooch? Whether he made the fake pot himself or not, the fact that he put these pots here means he knew."

They all looked at Gilbert, who seemed lost in thought, holding a shard of the plaster of paris in his hand. Finally he said, "He might have. But if it's a valuable piece of jewelry, why didn't he put it on display, or hide it in a bank vault, or sell it?"

"It wasn't his," Mason said gently. "Why else would he have hidden it?"

"My dad wasn't a thief," he said, looking Mason in the eye. But he didn't sound certain.

"He could have been holding it for a friend," Ned said, "and maybe he didn't even know there was something valuable there. Maybe a buddy told him, 'Keep these pots for me, and don't ask any questions.'"

"If it's something like that, it would have been a long time ago," Gilbert said. "Look at the dirt on the shards; these pots have been here for donkey's years. They've been stacked in the barn as long as I can remember."

"Well, we can't ask Daniel," Ned said.

"Sadly, no," said Gilbert, and threw the shard down. "And if there wasn't something hinky about it, I'd take it to the Jewelry District tomorrow and sell the damn thing. But you're right—it was hidden for a reason. Mason, can you figure this out?"

"I can look into it," Mason said, "but I can't promise I'll find anything."

Ned said, "Don't underestimate yourself. You found Miss Cassie's bougie daughter for her, and she'd been missing for years."

Gilbert nodded. "I'll pay you either way. I'm on unemployment right now, but there's some dough in my dad's estate that'll come to me. Ned's going to help me figure that out."

"So where are you going to start?" Peggy asked Mason as they walked back to the house.

"I guess I'll read the brooch, and see where that leads."

"I'm going to work in that groovy studio, but call me if you need some help."

Peggy lugged her guitar and her computer bag into the music room, and Ned and Gilbert sat at the messy desk in Daniel's cramped office. It showed Daniel's priorities, Mason thought, that he had used the smallest room for business, while his library and music spaces were much larger. He walked into the library and stood there for a minute, listening to the house. Peggy had shut the door to the music room, so there wasn't a sound from there, but he could hear Gilbert and Ned next door.

"Money has never made any sense to me," Gilbert was saying. "You'll have to start from zero.…"

He closed the door to tune them out. The brooch was sitting there on a bookshelf, all shiny, just waiting for him. He was hesitant to jump right into it, not because he was afraid the mystery was unsolvable—though he did think it might be— but because he knew it was probably the start of something that might consume all his time and energy for a while. It's OK to procrastinate for a few minutes, he told himself, but soon enough his curiosity overcame his inertia, and he picked the brooch up off the shelf. It was heavier than its size implied, like a thick-bottomed tumbler.

He sat in one of the two wingback armchairs and set the brooch on the armrest, looking at it for a few minutes. It really was beautiful. He pulled off his ring, not wanting it to interfere with his reading. He closed his eyes and started to push down all the random thoughts that popped into his mind, gradually creating a quiet, blank space. He picked up the brooch and held it in his left hand, covering it with his right. He waited for any image or feeling that might come up, hoping he could distinguish true insight from the random noise of his mind. He didn't have to wait long.

A strong image coalesced, becoming sharp and vivid. It startled him, like turning on a radio when the volume was set too loud. He saw a chamber with stone walls, and it was dark, lit only by flickering light; maybe candles or oil lamps. A woman stood with her back to him, her hands held up toward the wall. She seemed so real that it frightened him a little, but he held on to the image and took a deep breath, reminding himself to be calm. He focused on the woman. She was swaying rhythmically. Maybe she's performing a ritual, he thought. She wore a dark blouse and a loose knee-length skirt, and her black hair was roughly plaited down her back; he'd never seen anyone in that kind of getup before. She looked warm, her skin glistening with sweat. Slowly she started to turn around, arms still in the air. She was looking up, as if in a trance, her expression blank. As she turned, her dark eyes shifted downward, looking toward Mason. With a start he realized she was looking at him; he wasn't just observing her and the chamber from outside, he was there—and she could see him. She took a step toward him, stretching her arms out, her fingers spreading into claws, her face contorting into shrieking rage. Mason screamed and leaped out of the chair, throwing the brooch onto the carpet, where it landed with a clunk.

His heart was pounding in his ears, and he blinked and shook his head to make sure the vision was completely gone. He'd never seen anything that intense doing psychometry. He was breathing hard, trying to dissipate the rush of adrenaline, when Ned pushed open the library door. He looked at Mason for a moment, then looked down at the brooch on the floor.

"Everything OK?" he asked. "We heard a scream."

"Yeah, that was me. I'm all right. I just had a strange experience with the brooch."

"You threw it on the floor?"

"It almost felt alive for a second," he said. He wasn't going to tell Ned what had actually happened and invoke his disbelief, but he really had felt the brooch wiggle, or vibrate, in the moment just before he cast it down. But that was surely just his imagination, he thought, brought on by such a vivid psychic image.

"I see," Ned said, raising his eyebrows. "It

sounded pretty intense."

"I'm fine," Mason said firmly.

"I guess I'll leave you to it, then." He glanced around the room and pulled the door closed, leaving Mason alone again.

It must be nice to have it all figured out, Mason thought. Ned's skepticism was palpable, like a bad smell in the air.

He slipped his ring back on; it, at least, felt comfortingly inert. He looked down at the brooch on the carpet, lying there immutable. Who was that angry woman? The original owner? If so, it felt like a very long time ago. How many centuries had it been waiting to be dug up? The woman in the vision was terrifying. He might be able to find out who she was, but no way was he going to read that thing again.

The brooch probably won't bite if I touch it again, he thought, especially if I'm not trying to get information from it. He picked it up and set it back on the bookshelf without incident.

He went to the master bedroom to get his laptop, and brought it back to the library. He started digging around on the Web for "gold brooch" and "antique gold brooch," which brought up a lot of jewelry for sale, none of which looked anything like the piece Gilbert had found. He checked with a couple of museums that had photos of their artifacts online, but again nothing looked remotely familiar. He searched for "angry priestess" and then "angry queen," but that brought up dark-side wiccans, sassy drag performers, and even a news item about a beef among some minor European royalty. After a while he gave up and folded his laptop closed.

He opened the library door and looked in on Gilbert and Ned. They were huddled over a sheaf of paper, heads together. Gilbert looked up and said "Hey," but went back to reading.

"How are you doing?" Ned asked, concern in his eyes.

"All good," Mason said. "Taking a break." That look was enough to melt his lingering resentment. Even though Ned wasn't always supportive, he really did care about Mason.

Ned smiled and looked back to their paperwork.

The door to the music room was still closed. He hated to interrupt Peggy, but it was starting to feel like lunchtime, and Ned didn't look like he was going to do anything about it; she was the next best cook in the house. Maybe he could just look in on her through the window, he thought, and see how she was doing.

He went out the front door and walked around the side of the house. It was hard to see inside because it was so bright out. He cupped his hands to the first window past the patio and looked in, but it was one of the bedrooms, with Peggy's girl clothes strewn around. He cupped his hands at the next window, and there she was, sitting cross-legged on the floor, electronic components stacked around her, and cables running all over. She must have noticed him blocking the light, he realized, because she turned toward the window, a look of alarm on her face. Her eyes narrowed as she peered at him. He could just make out her muffled words through the glass.

"Mason, what the fuck?" she shouted, then gestured wildly toward the door.

He walked back around and inside, and pushed the music room door open.

"You scared the hell out of me," she said. "I thought it was the Sasquatch trying to break in."

"Sorry about that," he said. "I just wanted to see how you were doing without interrupting. I'm shocked—Peggy Pregnant has gone electronic."

"No, she hasn't," Peggy said. She and Mason had a longstanding debate about the value of electronic music; Mason loved it and embraced it, but Peggy believed that anything beyond a microphone and an amp diluted true music. "This is all equipment for recording actual music, not generating fake music. And it's really good equipment. Daniel knew what he was doing."

"Have you been laying down your beats?" he asked.

Peggy laughed. "I've mostly just figured out what everything is, and hooked it all up. But I'm definitely going to do some recording later on."

"More pressing than that is what we're going to do for lunch."

"Aw, is Mason getting hungry?"

"Yeah, and Ned is completely buried in paper in Daniel's office. I'm afraid to even walk past the doorway. There's some very heavy 'do not disturb' energy coming out of there."

"Well, let's make them some sandwiches with that faux turkey, and they can eat in there. But you have to help."

"Deal," he said.

Peggy delivered lunch to the office and then sat at the kitchen table with Mason to eat. "So did you read the pin?" she asked him.

"I did." He looked at her for a moment, and considered telling her the truth. But if her conscious mind couldn't handle the weirdness of passing their doppelgängers on the road, how would she react to him almost getting jumped in a psychic vision? "All I got was just some vague general vibes."

"What kind of vibes?" she asked, biting into her sandwich.

"Well, I think the thing is old—really old, like from antiquity."

"In that case, it'll be far more valuable than just the gold that's in it," she said.

"I guess. I looked around on the Web, but I couldn't find anything like it. I think the next step is library work, back in the city."

"Mason, think! You have a whole library right here," she said. "If Daniel knew about the pin, maybe he has a book about it."

"That's a good idea. I'll poke around in there

today, and see if anything jumps out." He looked at her for a moment. "How did you get to be so smart?"

"It's a congenital condition called double X-chromosome syndrome," she said.

It took him a moment to get what she was saying. "OK," he said, and smiled. "It must be a grind to be here with all these guys."

"Not at all. I'm enjoying myself." She shifted in her chair. "Listen, Mason, you know how we were talking about my half-brother, Andrew? I finally talked to him today."

"Peggy, that's huge."

"I think what Ned said motivated me—it's later than we think. So I called him, and we talked for a long time."

"What kind of guy is he?" Mason asked.

"He sounds pretty ordinary. He was kind of upbeat, but that might just be because he was talking to me. It's exciting for both of us. He lives in the close part of the Valley, and works in the film industry, with music, if you can believe that."

"It's not hard to believe. Your mutual parent was a musician."

"That's true—maybe it's genetic. He does scores for films and TV."

"Maybe he can get you some music gigs in the biz," Mason said, polishing off the last bite of his sandwich.

"That was my first thought too," she laughed, "but I'm not going to ask him about it until I know him better."

"Did you talk about meeting in person?"

"We did, and remember your thing about coincidences and synchronicity? It turns out that this is the weekend he opened his cabin, so he's up here right now too. I don't know where, exactly, but he's in the same nonexistent desert town as this place, so he has to be close."

"No way is that a coincidence," Mason said, amazed. "It has to be meaningful."

"Is that what 'synchronicity' actually implies?"

"Yeah. A coincidence is just random background noise, like it rained on the 15th last month, and it rained on the 15th this month. There's no connection, no meaning. But synchronicities have meaning, and maybe a reason for happening. The fact that you and your brother are both in the same dinky town on the same weekend, that's too meaningful to be a coincidence."

"Well, maybe the meaning is that we're supposed to meet. We're going to get together tomorrow—apparently there's an indie coffee joint back in the town where we bought the groceries."

"Wow. Are you nervous?"

"Big time. Actually, I was thinking it might be nice if you came with me. Ned and Gilbert are going to be working on Daniel's estate stuff, so maybe you and I can drive over there and check this guy out."

"I'd love to," Mason said. "I'm curious to see what he's like, whether he's like you."

"I wouldn't have even known he existed without you, so it seems appropriate that you come along on our first meeting. Maybe that's part of the synchronicity, that you're up here too."

"Does he have a partner or someone with him?"

"No, it's just him. I'm pretty sure he's single—he's never mentioned being married or partnered. I'm assuming it'll just be the three of us."

"Will it be weird for you to show up with a bodyguard?"

"Not at all—he knows you're my roommate, that you did the research to find him. I told him you'd probably come along."

After they'd cleaned up, Peggy cloistered herself in the music room once again, and Mason returned to the library. The brooch was there in its place on the bookshelf, its gleam and gravity hard to ignore. He couldn't fathom how Ned couldn't feel that. Even the possibility of psychic insight was too much of a challenge to Ned's scientific worldview. But infuriatingly, he had no trouble buying into Gilbert's aliens, which seemed even less scientific than psychometry. Maybe they would never understand each other.

He sighed and looked around the room. Daniel must have loved books, he thought, or maybe he just couldn't get rid of them. This certainly looked like a lifetime's worth. He looked at some of the shelves, trying to discern whether they were organized in any way, but there didn't seem to be any pattern; novels next to memoirs next to nonfiction, all jumbled together. There were some great old books, he realized, hardbound volumes dating back decades. He browsed for a while, reading snatches of various tomes here and there, trying not to get so engaged that he'd get distracted from his goal.

Eventually he stopped and sat in one of the wing chairs. There was no way to find anything except by looking at everything. Maybe there was some psychic trick he could use, he thought, a way to find out if there was a volume in this room that would give him a lead. He closed his eyes and spent some time clearing his mind. Finally, he said out loud, "Show me." He wanted the right book to call him, to invite him over to its shelf. He didn't feel anything specific, but he stood up, eyes still closed, turned, and slowly walked toward the shelves. He put out his hands and wriggled his fingers, eventually reaching out and settling on a book on a shelf at eye level. He couldn't say that the book had called to him, but it was the book that was in his hands now.

He opened his eyes and looked it over. It was dark red, hardbound, and old; the spine read THE LOST WEEKEND. He flipped to the copyright page. It had been printed in 1945. He wondered if it might have belonged to Gilbert's grandparents. He riffled through the yellowed pages, and a small square of paper fell out and fluttered to the floor.

He reached down and picked it up; it wasn't

paper, he saw, but a little piece of aluminum foil, about two inches square. Flipping carelessly through the book was stupid, he realized; if it had been a bookmark, now he'd never know what page it had been on. He sat down with the book and put the foil square on the arm of the chair. He read the first few pages. It was fiction, and not anything to do with jewelry, or antiquity, or angry priestesses. He set it aside and picked up the foil. It wasn't regular kitchen foil, as it had some kind of thin coating. When he wrinkled it or folded it, the foil would pop back to its original flatness, leaving no creases. Bizarre stuff. Maybe he could do psychometry on it, he thought, since it was made of metal. It was a stretch, but it was worth a try.

He pulled off his ring and set it on the arm of the chair. He closed his eyes again and pressed down the noise in his mind. "No angry people this time," he said out loud, then put the foil in one hand and covered it with the other. He waited for some images or feelings, but nothing came. Eventually he opened his eyes and looked at the foil again. "Nada," he said. It looked the same but felt quite warm now. It must have been from his body heat. He slipped his ring back on; it felt surprisingly cold in comparison.

Should he show it to Gilbert? It was an odd little thing, but it didn't seem important, and it hadn't told him anything. The most logical place for it was back in *The Lost Weekend.* He slipped it between the pages and slid the book back into its slot on the shelf. He looked around the room and sighed. Daniel's library was another dead end.

It was a great place to read, though, and he did need a break from thinking about the brooch. He flipped open his computer and got lost perusing the news. He thought of a few more ideas that might shed light on the brooch and did some searching, but nothing meaningful appeared. He even did some digging into Gilbert's father, "Daniel Quintero," which led him through pages about his company, Quintero Movers. It seemed like it was a bigger operation than the little family business Gilbert had described, and it was still going strong; Daniel must have sold it to someone at some point. The company's website showed a fleet of Quintero trucks parked in front of a commercial storage facility. Why hadn't Gilbert taken a role in the family business, he wondered? But knowing how flaky Gilbert could be, if he'd been in charge, he might have driven it into the ground.

Somewhere in the house, a doorbell rang. Curious, Mason opened the library door. Gilbert was coming out of the office.

"You expecting company?" Mason asked him.

"No," he said, and walked to the front of the house, Mason trailing behind him. He opened the door to a woman dressed in a plaid shirt and jeans. She was tall, Mason thought, maybe 5 foot 10, and dark, perhaps from lots of time outdoors, or maybe Native American or even South Asian heritage. She had extremely straight, dry-looking black hair. Fashion-wise, she definitely fit into the desert rat category.

"Laura Rain," Gilbert said. "I thought I saw your rig parked out there on the arroyo."

"That's me," she said, and shook his hand with both of hers.

"This is my friend Mason, from LA," he said.

Mason stepped toward her and extended a hand. "Hello," he said, and attempted a charming grin. "Did I hear your name correctly as 'Rain,' like R-A-I-N?"

She grasped his hand and looked him in the eye, cocking her head to one side. "Have we met before?"

"No, I don't think so," Mason said, slightly unnerved at the lengthy handshake. These desert people must not have much opportunity to develop social skills, he thought. "Unless you work at that supermarket back in the town."

"No." She let go of his hand but continued staring at him.

"Laura, would you like to come in for coffee?" Gilbert asked.

"Yes," she said, breaking her gaze with Mason and walking past him into the house. She sat at the kitchen table while Gilbert pulled coffee cups out of a cupboard.

"Mason?" he asked, waggling a coffee cup at him.

"Sure," he said.

Laura sat bolt upright in her chair, staring at Gilbert in the kitchen. Mason wasn't sure whether to engage with her or not, but finally he perched on the edge of one of the chairs, his hands on his knees.

"So, Laura, are you from around here, or just camping?" he asked her.

She turned her head to look at him. "Yes."

He nodded nervously; she was staring at him again, and again hadn't answered his question.

Ned walked in from the back of the house. "Hello," he said, eyeing the newcomer.

"Ned, this is Laura," Gilbert said. "She's the one who's camping out on the arroyo. Do you want coffee?"

"Sure," he said, and to Laura, "I'm Ned, a friend of Gilbert's from way back."

"Enchanté," she said, her voice almost sing-song.

Ned smiled and sat at the table across from her.

"I heard that Daniel had died," she said, as Gilbert passed the cups around and sat down with them, "and I wanted to …" she paused, and stared at him, expressionless. "To express my condolences."

"Thank you," he said. "It's only been a couple of days. I still can't believe that he's gone."

"Death isn't the end," she said simply.

Ned folded his arms and leaned back in his chair. Mason could see he was trying not to scowl.

He was almost certainly expecting her to start talking about angels, and heaven, and how Daniel was better off there; or worse, to start proselytizing. Ned knew there was no point in arguing with a religious person, but Mason knew he wasn't above getting into it.

"So you live in your trailer?" Ned asked, redirecting the conversation.

"I'm the one who's camping out on the arroyo. About twelve hundred meters due north."

"Are you European?" Ned asked, his eyes narrowing. "Or military? People in California don't use metric very much."

"I'm a scientist," she said, and smiled thinly.

Ned looked at Mason and raised his eyebrows, as if to say, "And here I thought she was a Jesus freak."

She turned to Mason again. "You're visiting from LA because of Daniel's death?"

"Uh, yes," he said. Why did this woman make him so uncomfortable? She wasn't warm and fuzzy, and seemed a little obtuse, but it was more than that. "I'm doing some research for Gilbert, and Ned is helping Gilbert go through Daniel's paperwork."

"You're using Daniel's library?" she said, her eyebrows rising inquisitively.

"Yes, in fact, I am. He certainly had a lot of books."

"And you're achieving your research goals?"

"Well, I just got started, so, not yet, no. But

I'm confident I can get some answers for Gilbert once I get back to the city."

"Sometimes the smallest things are important," she said, and smiled.

That's the first time she's acted like she's not on tranquilizers, he thought. But what the hell was she talking about? "I didn't really find any of his books relevant, although of course I didn't look at all of them," he said.

"No small things," she said.

"Sorry," Mason said, "but what do you mean?"

Laura didn't answer, but turned to look at Gilbert.

"Why don't you come for dinner this evening?" Gilbert asked her, a silly grin on his face. "Ned, are you up for cooking for five?"

"I guess I could do that," Ned said slowly, but he looked unsure.

"What time?" Laura asked.

"Maybe around seven?" Gilbert said, looking at Ned, who nodded.

"That's in four hours?" Laura asked.

"More like three," Gilbert said, pulling out his phone and checking its clock.

"Today, three hours from now," Laura said.

"Yes," Ned said. "But it'll be nighttime by then. Are you OK to walk back over here in the dark?"

"It won't be a problem," she said, and stood up. She hadn't touched her coffee.

Gilbert walked her to the front door and said

good-bye, then came back to the kitchen. "What a babe," he said.

Mason and Ned stared at him in stunned silence. Finally, Ned said, "Are you kidding?"

"There's just something about her. She's hot."

"Do you have history with her?" Mason asked. "Because it seems like there's something going on that I'm missing."

"I met her up here a while ago. She used to drop in on my dad. I thought we had a connection, you know, even though we never really went out," he said, staring out at the landscape, remembering. "And then one day, I saw her in a diner in town, and she acted like we'd never met. She completely ignored me—just sat there with her orange juice." His eyes smoldered.

"OK, then," Ned said, looking concerned. Clearly he didn't want Gilbert to get upset again, as he had that morning. "If we're eating in a few hours, I'm going to do some food prep now. We've done enough of the estate stuff for one day, don't you think?"

"Yeah, let's take a break. Mason, you want to go smash stuff with a baseball bat?"

"That sounds more like a straight-guy kind of thing, but I'll try anything once," Mason said. "Unless you want some kitchen help?" he asked Ned.

"Go," Ned said, rising from the table and waving his hand dismissively.

In the barn, Mason picked up a stack of the

terra-cotta pots, then set them outside in the corral. Gilbert swung the bat around in the air a few times, warming up, and then took the batter's stance a few feet away.

"Throw it high, and I'll hit it as it falls," he said.

Mason picked up a pot, and with both hands swung it down between his legs and up into a high arc toward Gilbert. Gilbert swung the bat and connected with the pot with a loud *crack*. Chunks of terra-cotta flew, and Mason held out his arm and squinted to keep the detritus out of his eyes.

"Another?" Mason asked, but Gilbert had already started swinging at the larger shards on the ground, pounding them repeatedly, swinging with both hands, grunting with the effort. It was primal, Mason thought, unbridled rage. When there was nothing left but red powder, Gilbert stood erect. He was panting, his eyes were wild, and he had a lopsided grin on his face.

"I want to try that," Mason said.

Gilbert handed him the bat and he got into a ready position, shifting his weight back and forth between his feet.

"You're holding the bat too low," Gilbert said. "Hold it up by your shoulders."

Mason made the adjustment, and Gilbert threw a pot for him. He swung just a little too late and struck it with a glancing blow, but it was enough to shatter it.

"Yeah!" Gilbert shouted.

Mason pounded the shards into rubble, with less zeal than Gilbert, but still, it felt great.

"My turn," Gilbert said, and took the bat.

"So what is it about Laura that you find so attractive?" Mason asked, and threw a pot for him.

Crack! Gilbert didn't answer until he had pulverized all the bits of terra-cotta. "Well," he said, breathing hard, "I have this … feeling for her. It's not like I want to smooch that cooch," he said, and Mason struggled not to visualize that, "but it's more like I want to take care of her, or help her out." He handed Mason the bat.

"It sounds like a romantic crush," Mason said, but he couldn't really understand what he saw in her. He wondered if more would be revealed at dinner. He'd never really trusted Gilbert, but he could see that he was being forthright, which was a way of being honest. Maybe he was developing some respect for the guy.

As the pot spun toward him, Mason flashed to the image of the angry woman in his vision in the library, enraged, reaching out for him. He hesitated, and the bat whiffed the air, the pot tumbling unbroken to the ground.

"You're balking," Gilbert said. "Keep your eyes on the prize."

They spent another half hour smashing up more pots, egging each other on and congratulating each other on the powdery red destruction. Finally Gilbert said, "I'm overheating," and they went back into the house. Mason found Ned sprawled on the master bed, immobile but not asleep. He climbed on beside him, and Ned rolled over to put his arm across Mason's chest.

"There's grit on your shirt," Ned said.

"I tried to brush it off, but I must have missed some."

"Was it fun?"

"Extremely. Gilbert says I have good hand-eye coordination. And hey, that was nice of you to agree to cook for his guest."

"I would have been cooking anyway. It's why I'm here, right, to do whatever to help out. I also think having a female to fixate on is a good distraction. He can talk about the loss, and he is talking about it as we're sorting through his dad's estate, but at least there's something else to do too."

"How is that going, by way?"

"The estate? There's a lot more there than he expected. It's going to have to go to probate."

Mason had no idea what that meant, but said, "That makes sense." He turned toward him and ran his hand through Ned's thick hair. "I must say, what you're doing for Gilbert is admirable."

"He and I have a lot of history, and I can't imagine it any other way. It's like when you're traveling in Spain, and you're the only one who speaks Spanish—you just do it. Or like when you and I go clothes shopping. I'm the only one who can save you from yourself."

"Funny," Mason said, "and yet there's a kernel of truth there." His arm was against Ned's chest, and he could feel his heart beating. "I'm looking forward to dinner. I think Gilbert has a crush on that woman."

"There's definitely something going on," Ned said. "I've never seen him like that. Usually when he's on the make, he's very suave, and persistent, but with her he seems lost."

"She's just so bizarre—what does he see in her? I can't really get a read. I wondered if she was on something, but I couldn't figure out what kind of drugs would make you that way. What's that one where people commit sleep crimes?"

"Ambien."

"Right. Maybe she's on an Ambien sleepwalking trip."

A WHILE LATER MASON had a shower and then offered to help Ned, who had returned to the kitchen.

"You could give Peggy a heads-up about what's going on," Ned said. "She's been locked up in the music room all afternoon."

Mason didn't want to interrupt her recording, if that was what she was doing, and thought about going back out to her window; but that had frightened her before. Finally he decided to send her a text message. He pulled out his phone and thumb-typed:

News! Laura is coming for dinner. Do you have an evening gown with you?

Within seconds Peggy had burst out of the music room and found Mason in the kitchen. "What did I miss?" she demanded. They sat at the kitchen table, and Mason briefed her on Laura's visit, with Ned chiming in with details as he worked behind the counter.

"I'm excited to meet her," Peggy said. "What was she wearing?"

Mason said, "A plaid blouse and jeans. She was working kind of a lumberjack look."

"She wasn't working a look, she was just wearing what people wear when they go camping," Ned said.

"So I wonder if I should dress up," Peggy said.

"I'm sure she won't," Ned said. "She's camping out there, remember?"

"I'm not so sure. This is a house full of guys, and I know women," Peggy said.

NED HAD MASON SET cutlery and napkins and glasses on the table outside on the patio, and haul a kitchen chair out to make room for five. It was almost dark out, the sky glorious pink and purple around the horizon, but the patio had lighting, and in such a dry climate there weren't any insects to bother them. Mason looked out toward the arroyo for any sign of Laura approaching, but couldn't see anything moving.

Close to seven, Gilbert emerged from his bedroom. He looked like a new man—his hair neatly slicked back, and he was clean-shaven; Mason had never seen him without a few days' stubble. He wore dress pants and a white collared shirt. Ned was carrying a pitcher toward the patio doors but stopped when he saw Gilbert, and looked him up and down.

"Jesus, Gilbert. Do you have a corsage for her too?" Ned asked him. "You know no one else is going to dress up, right?"

At that moment Peggy walked into the kitchen. She wasn't really dressed up, Mason thought, but she'd changed into a pretty color-block top and a short summer skirt.

"Great," Ned said. "Now I have to put on a decent shirt too." He handed Mason the pitcher and said, "Soba dipping sauce. It goes on the table," and strode off into the back of the house.

"I guess that leaves me the only one dressed like an oaf," Mason said.

"That's a good thing," Gilbert said. "Less competition for me."

When the doorbell rang, Gilbert jumped like he'd had an electric shock and hurried to the front door. Mason pulled out his phone to look at the time; it was exactly seven o'clock. He and Peggy followed Gilbert to the door.

Laura was transformed. Gone was the camping drag—now she wore a simple knee-length black dress with two strands of pearls. She was indeed curvy, as Gilbert had said.

"This is Mason and Ned's roommate, Peggy, from the city," Gilbert said, looking only at Laura.

"Peggy, this is Laura."

"How do you do," Laura said, and Peggy grasped her hand and leaned in for an air kiss.

"This way," Gilbert said, and led her to the patio.

Peggy hung back and whispered to Mason, "I knew she'd outdress me. I just knew it."

"How could you have known that?" Mason said quietly.

"It's a chick thing. We've never met, so of course she'd bring her A game."

"OK," Mason said, mystified. "But doesn't it seem weird that she'd have an outfit like that on a camping trip?"

They were walking out onto the patio, so Peggy didn't reply. They sat around the table, and Gilbert went back into the kitchen, returning a moment later with a bottle of wine in each hand. "Red or white?" he asked Laura.

"Oh … either one," she said, so Gilbert poured red. Normally people have a preference, Mason thought. But despite that, she seemed more present, more focused than she'd been earlier in the day.

"So, Laura, do you flat-iron your hair? It looks lovely," Peggy said. It didn't, Mason knew; it looked like charred straw. He wasn't sure if Peggy was being catty or not.

"No," Laura said, reaching up and feeling her hair. "It came this way."

Peggy laughed. "Mine too. Straight hair is like

a blank canvas. I can do anything I want with it."

Ned stepped out onto the patio. He'd changed into a lovely dark-blue fitted shirt and black trousers. It really did leave Mason the only one casually dressed, in a T-shirt and shorts, but he pushed the concern away; he knew it didn't really matter.

Ned did a double-take when he saw Laura. "You clean up nicely," he said, and stepped around the table to give her an air kiss.

"Thank you," she said.

Gilbert poured soda water for Ned and red wine for Peggy and Mason, then said, "A toast: to new friends." They clinked glasses, but Mason noticed that Laura didn't drink.

"So, the four of us are Angelenos," Ned said. "Laura, where did you grow up?"

"I'm from Portland," she said.

Ned and Peggy both said, "Oh," at the same time, as if that explained everything.

"I love it up there," Ned said.

"Yeah, great food," Gilbert added.

They talked about Portland, and then about LA, and then about Natron and the Mojave. Laura didn't say much, but chimed in often enough that it wasn't awkward.

Gilbert split the last of the red wine between his and Peggy's glasses, then said, "I'm getting tipsy, Nedly. Where's the chow?"

"I'm on it," Ned said, and sprang up. Dinner was a chopped salad, cold soba noodles, and asparagus spears, with a sauce for each.

"How do you do this?" Gilbert asked, marveling at the spread.

"It's not that much work once you know what you're doing," Ned said.

"Well, thanks for doing it," Gilbert said, diving in.

Mason watched Laura surreptitiously as they ate. She twirled some soba noodles around her fork, and pushed the salad around her plate, but she never took a bite. Was she anorexic? He looked at Peggy and Ned, but neither of them seemed to have noticed. Gilbert was watching her, but he was in her thrall; nothing she did would have seemed odd to him.

"So where did you go to school, Laura?" Peggy asked.

"Portland," she said, and then, "I have to pee," and abruptly stood up and walked into the house.

"OK, then," Peggy said, once she was out of earshot. "I'm glad we cleared that up."

"Meow," Ned said to her, and laughed. "I guess you can put the desert rat in a little black dress, but she'll still be a desert rat."

"You're being classist," Gilbert said. "She has to pee; what of it? Everybody pees, *cabrón*. There's nothing ratty about it."

"I didn't say there was," Ned protested.

Peggy said, "Did you see how she was playing with her food? I think she's bulimic, and she's gone to woof up her dinner." She set her napkin on the table and said, "You know what? I'm just going to go listen at the bathroom door to see."

"No!" Gilbert said, shocked. "Leave her alone."

"Aren't you at least a little curious?" she said.

"She didn't eat anything," Mason said. "Am I the only one who noticed that? Look at her plate. There's nothing in her stomach to bring up."

"I'm still going to go listen," Peggy said.

"Come on, *chica*," Gilbert said.

"At least let me do it," Mason said. Before Peggy could protest he got up and walked into the house. He had no intention of listening at the bathroom door, but he wanted to save Peggy the embarrassment of getting caught doing that. He walked into the back of the house until he was out of sight of the patio, planning to cool his heels for a minute and then go back out. But he saw that the bathroom door was wide open, the room dark. Where had she gone? He stood in the hall, staring at the doorway, considering the possibilities. Suddenly he heard someone breathing behind him, and he whirled around, startled. Laura was standing there, not three feet away, her expression blank.

"Uh … did you find the powder room?"

"Yes," she said, not embarrassed at all. She walked past him without another word, back through the kitchen toward the patio.

Mason took a deep breath to calm himself. He thought for a moment. Where had she been? She might have had time to use the bathroom and then go exploring, but he doubted it. He stepped into the bathroom and flipped on the light; the sink was dry, so she hadn't washed her hands. That might not be unusual for someone used to camping in the desert. But the toilet seat was flipped up, meaning Gilbert had been the last one to use it; living with a woman, Mason and Ned were in the habit of always putting it down. Laura had clearly lied about having to pee.

He had a sudden thought: the brooch. His heart pounding, he walked back down the hall to the library and pushed open the door. The light was on—she must have been in here, because he always turned it off. But the brooch was still there, right where he'd left it. He walked over and looked at it closely. He hesitated to pick it up, still traumatized by the angry woman in the weird clothes that he'd seen when he'd read it—but he had to, just to be sure.

Its heft was unmistakable. Such a pretty thing, he thought, admiring its delicate swirls for a moment. He put it back on the bookshelf and found an old magazine to cover it up with. It wasn't much of a security measure, but at least now it was out of sight. Gold had been known to make people do strange things.

As he took his seat at the table again, Gilbert was telling a story about his father. He was less upbeat now, more subdued. Ned went into the kitchen and returned with a bowl of raspberries and a stack of little dishes.

"Raspberries are a treat," Peggy said.

"They remind me of you, Mason," Ned said, spooning raspberries into his dish. "Raspberry-red lips, red earlobes when you're embarrassed." He looked across the table at Mason and smirked. "And with your shirt off, raspberry-red nipples."

"Ned, we're eating," Peggy said.

"Show us, Mason," Gilbert said, leering.

"Absolutely not," Mason said, and felt his cheeks burning.

Laura looked at Mason and said, "So where did you and Ned meet?"

Interesting that she picked up that they were a couple, he thought, but then it dawned on him that that's what Ned was trying to do, letting her know they weren't in circulation. Mason looked down at the table and nodded, as if deep in thought. "We met at a dinner party, when I was at Vassar," he began. "Ned came up from the city to visit some friends. They thought I was just this snob from Newport...."

Gilbert's brow furrowed. "That's not right," he said.

Laura looked from Mason to Gilbert, and Ned chuckled.

"It's not his story," Peggy explained. "It's Jackie O's story."

"Was Jackie O your previous boyfriend?" Laura asked Ned. Mason laughed loudly, but then realized she wasn't kidding.

"Uh, no," Ned said, and shrugged, clearly at a loss.

Laura didn't say anything, but took her napkin from her lap and delicately dabbed at her lips. Why does she bother, Mason wondered, when she didn't eat anything? When she set the napkin down, her mouth looked different. He couldn't quite put his finger on it, but it was like her mouth was shaped differently now. She must have wiped off some of her lipstick, he realized. He looked at Peggy, who had seen it too; she looked startled.

"I think it's time to be going," Laura said, and stood up.

"Well, it's been lovely to spend some time with you," Gilbert said. They all said good-bye, and as Gilbert walked her to the door, Mason heard him saying, "You know, I'll be here for a few more days...."

"Did you see the lip thing?" Peggy asked as soon as they were gone.

"I did," Mason said. "She must have wiped off her lipstick."

"She wasn't wearing lipstick," Peggy said. "I noticed that when she came in. She has great skin, but no makeup on at all. When she wiped her lips," she said, leaning forward, "her lips wiped off."

"What are you talking about?" Ned said. "It must have been makeup."

"Maybe. But if so, there were no lips underneath. I swear—she wiped her lips off. There was nothing left on that side of her face."

"Maybe she had extremely thin lips?" Mason ventured.

"Maybe," Peggy conceded. "Or maybe her lips got burned off in an accident or something. But I tell you, that's one freaky chick. Mason, did you hear her purging?"

"No."

Ned said, "And who doesn't know who Jackie O is? Did she grow up under a rock?"

"Maybe she was pulling your leg, the way Mason was joking with her," Gilbert said, stepping back onto the patio.

"I guess that's possible," Ned said.

Mason considered telling them about finding her in the hallway, but decided against it. He knew Gilbert wouldn't be receptive to anything that might cast suspicion on her. But he did ask, "What was her connection to your dad? Were they friends?"

"He said he helped her out once in a while, when she needed help. I don't know what kind of help—I didn't ask. He was a little cagey about it, now that I think about it."

"Were they sleeping together?" Ned asked.

"No, I don't think it was that," Gilbert said.

"Maybe that's why she blew you off that time," Mason said.

"What happened?" Peggy asked. "I don't think I heard about that."

"A while back, I spent some time with her here at the house. I thought we had a groove going, but later, when I saw her in town, she acted like she didn't know who I was."

"How rude," Peggy said.

"I know. But now she's warmed up again, so maybe there's a chance."

"Gilbert, you're smitten," she said. "But do you really think she's into you? She seemed stand-offish to me."

"I honestly don't know," he said.

Mason said, "I'd tread carefully. My intuition tells me she's hiding something." It wasn't really a lie, he told himself, because he had found her skulking around the house, and from that he could intuit hidden motives.

"I don't know about that," Gilbert said, frowning.

"Gilbert, if anyone else had snubbed you in a diner like that, you'd think they'd secretly been replaced by a military robot, or brainwashed by a cult. But you've got a blind spot with this woman because you're into her."

He just said, "Yeah, maybe," and folded his arms.

"I think we all agree that she's unusual," Ned said, "but I don't know if that translates into dangerous. I think she's just a typical desert rat, with limited social skills."

"She was overdressed, though, which doesn't seem like a desert rat. And she grew up in Portland," Peggy said.

Gilbert said, "OK, people. I need to take some quiet time for myself this evening, so I'm going to retire. In case you're wondering, I'm not leaving because you're talking trash about my future girl-friend." He attempted a weak smile. "Can I help clean up?"

"I'll do that. You go chill," Mason said.

When he'd left, Peggy said, "He's completely besotted."

"Bewitched," Ned said glumly. "I miss the old Gilbert."

"Listen, boys," Peggy said, "I'm going to take my leave as well. I'm making progress with my music, and I want to spend some more time in the studio before bed. I hope I'm not being too antisocial?"

"Not at all," Ned said. "Have you started recording yourself?"

"Yeah, and I'm writing. When you can hear what you just wrote, it gives you better perspective, and it goes faster. I may have enough for an EP."

"That would be cool," Ned said. "I'd love to hear it when you're ready."

She smiled. "You'll be the first."

Mason helped Ned clear the table and clean up the kitchen. "So I'm not alone in thinking Gilbert is being delusional? That woman gave no indication she was interested in him at all."

"I know," Ned said. "It's sad, actually. But maybe he needs the distraction from his dad."

"There's something going on with her, but I can't put my finger on what it is."

"Well, she's Gilbert's problem, not yours. He

asked you to help him with the pin, but not with Laura. So we can marvel at her weirdness, but it's none of our business."

"I guess," Mason said, but he wasn't sure about that at all.

Ned changed out of his dress clothes into shorts and a T-shirt, and he and Mason sprawled on the master bed. Ned found the remote and clicked the TV on.

"Gilbert said they gave up TV service a while ago," he said, "but apparently there are still some over-the-air channels."

"I'm glad they didn't give up Internet," Mason said. He was engrossed in his laptop, reading about jewelry in antiquity. There was a lot to digest; every civilization that had access to gold made art and jewelry out of it, but he wasn't finding anything that looked like Gilbert's brooch.

Ned fiddled with the remote and found a channel that had an old movie playing, which seemed to satisfy him; he turned the volume low, set the remote aside, and picked up his tablet.

"What movie is this?" Mason asked.

"Who knows? I can't see a way to get program information. It's like living in the 1960s."

"It's definitely a 1960s movie, based on the outfits." Mason went back to his computer, looking up now and then to see what was happening in the film. It seemed to be a caper, with people running around Europe. As the Web searches

became more tedious, he spent more time looking at the TV. "Is that Ann-Margaret?" he asked.

Ned looked up. "Totally."

"How did they get her hair so high?"

"You know how sardines come in those flat
little cans? They'd put an empty sardine can under
her hair, and then comb it up around the can."

"Seriously?"

"Dead serious. And if there was a big event,
like a wedding, they'd use a soup can to get the
hair even higher."

"How do you know these things?"

"Look at her hair, man. Can there be any other explanation?"

Eventually Mason realized he was tired. He
considered initiating sex with Ned, to make himself feel better about getting upset with him earlier
in the day, but it felt a bit weird to do that in Daniel's house. Gilbert wouldn't care, he decided, but
Mason had been up early, and he'd had a decent
workout smashing terra-cotta. "I'm going to leave
you to the charms of Ann-Margaret," he said.
"Sleepy time for me."

"The TV won't bother you?"

"No. I'm exhausted. Just don't leave it on all
night." He rolled over, and rapidly felt the hypnagogic state coming on. Before drifting off he
gave himself the suggestion to have a lucid dream.
Wake up in it, he told himself.

At one point he realized that he was dreaming,
and felt elated at the awareness. He was looking

at a stretch of open water, maybe a harbor. It was a beautiful sunny day. He thought about trying to manipulate the dream, but decided just to watch, mindfully, to see what unfolded. A hovercraft raced across the water, followed by another identical one. They chased each other, never quite catching up, never slowing down. It seemed less than significant, and certainly shed no light on the mystery of the brooch. He didn't bother to will himself awake to write it down, but told himself to remember the images, and then drifted into deeper sleep.

BANG! MASON AWOKE WITH a start, at first not sure if the noise was in a dream or in the real world. Adrenaline flooded his body; it had definitely been in the house, and it had been loud. An explosion, or maybe an earthquake? The room was completely dark, and he felt around on the nightstand for the lamp. He clicked it on, winced at the light, and looked at his phone. 3:21 a.m.

Ned was still sound asleep. Mason grabbed his shoulder and shook him. "Ned! Did you hear that?" Ned's head lolled to one side, but his eyes didn't even flicker. "What's wrong with you? It sounded like someone broke down the front door." He felt Ned's neck for a pulse—at least he was alive.

What if the sound was someone breaking in? But Gilbert left the place unlocked, so an intruder could just walk in the front door without making a noise. And who would come all the way out here, in the middle of nowhere, to break into a house? He thought for a moment. Laura had been strolling around the place audaciously at dinner. The thought of her and her distorted lips prowling around the darkened house made him shiver.

He took a few deep breaths, to try to calm down. He listened to the house, straining to hear any sound, but there was nothing beyond the thump of his own heartbeat.

Maybe Peggy and Gilbert had woken up. He didn't want to leave the safety of the room, but after pulling on some clothes and glancing one last time at his boyfriend, he walked softly to the door. He turned the knob gingerly, trying not to make any sound, and pulled it open. He went out into the hallway and stood there, listening for movement, but there was only silence. In the dim glow, he could see that both Peggy's and Gilbert's doors were closed.

He walked toward the kitchen, as quietly as possible, but there was no one there, and not in the front room either when he peered in. The front door was intact and closed, and so was the one to the patio. What had made that huge sound?

He took a deep breath and went back down the hallway, to the library. He grabbed the knob and in a quick movement thrust open the door and snapped on the light. He squinted in the sudden brightness, but nothing looked disturbed. Scanning the room, nothing was out of place, including the magazine covering the brooch. Just to be sure, he looked under it. The brooch gleamed back at him, timeless and untouched.

Back in the nearly dark hallway he paused again, listening, but there wasn't a sound. He looked into the music room, also empty and undisturbed, and then poked his head into Gilbert's bedroom. He could hear the regular breathing of deep sleep, but he turned on the room light anyway. Gilbert was sprawled on top of the sheets, shirtless but mercifully wearing a pair of boxer shorts.

"Gilbert, did you hear that?" he said softly. Gilbert didn't stir. Mason watched him for a moment, then decided not to try to wake him.

Peggy was wound up in the sheets when he opened her bedroom door. "Peggy, did you hear that?" he said, but she didn't budge. He flipped on her light as well, to no response, and went over to her bedside. Her chest rose and fell in the rhythm of deep sleep.

"Am I the only light sleeper?" he said, and went back into the hallway, flipping off her light and closing the door behind him. Why had none of them heard it? It had been so loud. But there was no sign that it had come from inside the house. He stood in the hallway again, listening. Had he dreamed it? "Wake up," he said under his breath, as he had in Miss Cassie's office, his voice harsh in the quiet of the night.

He went back into the kitchen, to the patio

doors, and looked out. It was too dark to see the landscape, but some distance away was a point of white light. It was right about where they had seen Laura's trailer. She was either still awake, doing who knows what, or she had left a light on all night. At least she wasn't creeping around Daniel's house.

Staring at the dot of light, he thought about last night's dinner. Who comes to a dinner party and doesn't eat anything? The thought of it irritated him. And Ned was right—who would have grown up in Portland and never heard of Jackie O?

In a flash of insight, he realized that the explosion was somehow connected to Laura. He didn't know if she'd caused it, or why he would have heard it so sharply when her rig was so far away, but he knew, suddenly, that it involved her.

He knew what he had to do: walk over there and find out what she was up to. Why was the light on, and was she blowing stuff up? He didn't trust her, or her intentions, but because he'd been entrusted with the mystery of the brooch, and she'd been sneaking around in the library, he had to follow this lead. It was terrifying, because he had no idea what he'd find, but he had to go.

He rubbed sleep out of his eyes and went back into the master bedroom, sitting on the side of the bed to put on his orange sneakers. He moved quietly so as not to wake Ned, but he was still out cold. Mason eyed his phone, but the battery was low, and he decided to leave it.

He slid open the glass door to the patio, walked a few feet out from the house, and waited; he had been backcountry camping a few times, and he knew his eyes would adjust to the light, no matter how little there was. There was no moon, but gradually the stars seemed to brighten, and he started to see a vague gray texture to the landscape.

The wilderness began at the end of Daniel's concrete patio. He set off at a confident pace, skirting the infrequent shrubs, which loomed up as gray blobs in the darkness, heading toward the light in the distance at Laura's trailer. It was easy walking, once he could see; there wasn't a lot of ground cover, and the earth was hard-packed, not soft under his feet. He'd expected something like beach sand, seeing as this was a desert, but it was nothing like that. Walking took a lot of patience, he thought; if he'd been on his bicycle, he'd be there already.

He realized now that the light was bright blue, not white. He didn't look at it directly, so as to protect his night vision, but as he got closer it started to illuminate the landscape. Its growing proximity made his heart pound faster, and despite feeling exposed, he maintained his pace. Keep your eyes on the prize, like Gilbert said, he told himself.

It was odd, he thought, how Ned was in such a deep sleep, and the others too. It was almost like they were switched off. Maybe it was like seeing their doppelgängers on the road: they just couldn't handle it, so their minds protected them from it by shutting down. Mason still couldn't explain that bizarre episode, but he could handle it, and he was sure it had really happened. But if that experience, and this hike across the desert, were meant for him alone, why didn't he have a better sense of what was going on?

The light must have been on top of Laura's trailer, and even as he got closer its glare obliterated any view he might have of her vehicle. As it grew brighter, he started to feel more afraid. He thought of Laura silently sneaking up behind him, as she had in the hall, and then the contorted rage of the woman in the brooch vision invaded his mind again. What was he getting himself into? But he certainly couldn't turn back now, after walking all the way out here. He squinted to keep the light out of his eyes, but short of holding his hand in front of his face, it was impossible.

Finally he was almost on it, less than fifty feet away. He could see the curved roof of the Airstream. There didn't seem to be any lights in the windows, but if Laura was awake, she could certainly see him now. He walked closer. The soil here on the arroyo was coarse and sandy, like the desert of his imagination, and crunched under his sneakers.

There was a noise, he realized, a low hum, almost imperceptible, but when he focused on it he could hear it. It got stronger, then weaker, in a rhythmic pattern. Focusing on it, the pattern repeated about once every two seconds. It was calming, and he closed his eyes to listen for a moment. It was almost a different sound on each side of his head, like a stereo signal. But that was impossible. He tried to listen carefully, to analyze it, but it wasn't easy. It was the middle of the night, for one thing, but also he just couldn't wrap his mind around it.

He opened his eyes a little, squinting at the light, the hulking curves of Laura's rig below it. The shape seemed odd in the glare, like the perspective was off, the curves in the wrong places for an Airstream. The hum was throbbing now, more than a sound, almost a feeling. Maybe if he sat down for a minute he could figure it out.

He sat cross-legged, facing the light. The sand was really comfortable, he realized, like a nice sofa. He closed his eyes again and did a neck roll to loosen the muscles, focusing on the hum again. It's calming, he thought. I wonder what it is. I should probably look into it. I'm so lucky it's warm out here.

Sunday

"WHY DID YOU DO that?"

Mason started awake, and looked around groggily. Who had said that? It was loud, right up in his face, a woman's voice, but there was no one around. He blinked and rubbed his eyes, sitting up.

He was still out on the arroyo, the sun just above the horizon, casting brilliant pinks and purples around the rim of the sky. Laura's rig was gone. He rolled onto his knees and brushed the gravelly sand off his arms. He'd fallen asleep out here, and hadn't even heard her leave. How stupid, to walk all the way out here and then fall asleep. What had happened? All he remembered was the blue light guiding him across the landscape.

He stood up and stretched his back; he felt surprisingly well rested, considering he was never awake at this hour. Maybe it was being out in the breaking daylight. He looked around at the ground and couldn't even find Laura's tire tracks. Maybe she had been parked farther away from where he had crashed. But the wellhead that Gilbert had mentioned was here. It was an old-fashioned mechanical pump, set in a little concrete pad, and sure enough when he pushed it through a few strokes, water gushed out for a few seconds. He washed his face and wet his hair; in this desert climate it would dry in minutes, even though the air was still cool from the night. He drank deeply, then stood up and looked around. He couldn't see Daniel's house, which seemed odd. It had to be there. He knew the direction it was in based on the lay of the land, and he set off walking.

Eventually he could see the barn in the distance, but not the house. It must be obscured behind the barn, he reasoned, even though that didn't make sense; he should be able to see the house and the cars on this side of the barn. He had a flash of panic, thinking that he had come in the wrong direction, that this was some other barn, and he stopped to survey the horizon. No, this was exactly right; the mountains were in the right configuration, he was walking the right way.

He continued on toward the barn, and as he came up on it, he saw that it was indeed Daniel's barn: the shape of the roof, the weathered wood, and the broad door. But the house and the cars were nowhere to be seen. The road came up from the right direction, but where the house had been was just open land. It didn't make any sense. Somehow, he'd miscalculated. This had to be a different barn, a different road. But in his heart he knew it wasn't.

He walked up to the barn, looking over his shoulder in case Daniel's house might really be there if he looked away, with Ned just waking up to make breakfast, but no, it just wasn't there. He pulled open the barn door. There was nothing there, no horse tack, no terra-cotta pots or red dust, and no baseball bat. It hadn't been used for horses, smashing pots, or anything else for a long time.

He went back outside and walked over to where the house should have been. Standing about where the kitchen had been, he looked across the landscape. The view was the same as it had been yesterday: the arroyo and the distant mountains.

His hands felt cold despite the growing warmth from the sun. Maybe it was some kind of physical response; he closed his eyes and felt it in his back too, a rising cold, panicky feeling. But he had to keep his head, and figure this out. He walked back to the corral fence and sank down in the dirt, his back against one of the posts, staring at the place where the house had been. He pushed the cold feeling down and spent a few minutes breathing deeply, clearing his mind.

He thought back over the previous evening. A noise, he remembered, that was why he'd gone out there; he'd heard a noise, a loud bang. He thought it was connected to Laura, so he'd tramped across the landscape to where she was camping. He remembered the blue light, but it was fuzzy, like remembering a dream. And then he woke up to a shout. That must have been a vivid dream, someone shouting at him, enough to wake him up.

But none of that explained why Daniel's house wasn't here. Laura was gone, but she couldn't have towed it away with her. And anyway, it looked like the structure had never been there. Shrubs and plants had clearly been growing there for years. There were no tire tracks either, just the rutted dirt road, as if no vehicle had been this way in a long time. The sight of it all brought the clammy cold feeling back.

He had to stay calm, and not jump to any conclusions until he had the right information. Stay in the moment, he told himself, and don't freak out. He focused again on slowing down his breathing. What had Miss Cassie said about dreaming? How do you know you're not dreaming now? He knew he wasn't dreaming; it was never as vivid as reality. Doing psychometry on Gilbert's golden brooch, however, had produced a terrifyingly vivid image. Maybe he had opened himself up to psychic insight so much that he'd lost track of reality. He closed his eyes for a moment and said, "Wake up." But it was an unlikely possibility, and he knew nothing would change when he opened his eyes. This was no dream.

He wished he had his notepad to write things down on, but it was in the missing house, so his mind would have to suffice. He needed to make an interim plan to cope with this. First, don't freak out. Next, don't jump to any conclusions about what's going on or where Ned is. It might all become clear at any moment. Maybe this was some kind of special information, something important and otherworldly for him to figure out. But what the hell did it mean? This wasn't anything like reading a piece of jewelry and picking up some mental images.

There was nothing here; the only logical course of action was to get back to LA. It was only a mile back to the highway, and even though he'd never done it before, he was certain someone would stop for him if he stuck out a thumb to hitchhike. He stood up, swatted the dust off his butt, and started off down the road. He looked back once more to make absolutely sure it was still just the barn, but then shifted focus to getting out to the highway.

The day still hadn't heated up significantly, so he was able to move at a brisk pace. And thankfully, the highway was still there. It was extremely quiet; from the time he spotted it in the distance, not a vehicle went by until he was just a hundred yards away, when an old sedan roared past, headed north. Ned would love that, he thought, a 1960s boat in such good shape. He felt a twinge of sadness at the thought of Ned, and worry about where he was. Not having his phone with him meant he couldn't even call him if he wanted to; he had no idea what Ned's cell number was. He also didn't have his keys or his wallet, which meant no money, no cards, no ID. Ned, Peggy, his whole life was in that missing house, and if it didn't exist anymore … but the idea was too awful. He forced his mind back to the present. Don't freak out—that was the first rule.

He stepped up onto the pavement and walked across to the southbound side of the road. It was hard to believe a highway could be so dead, even in the middle of the desert, even this early in the morning on a Sunday. He looked north for any sign of an approaching vehicle, but the ribbon of asphalt stretched to the horizon with nothing moving on it. He started walking south, treading in the dust well to the side of the pavement. Caltrans wasn't too worried about safety margins out here, it seemed, as there wasn't even a white line at the side of the road, just pavement ending in dirt. His stomach rumbled. Food was going to become an issue at some point.

Before long he heard a motor in the distance behind him. Sure enough, a boxy brown car was bearing down on him. He took a deep breath and stuck out his thumb, and damn if it didn't slow down and pull up alongside him. It was another vintage vehicle, a flat-fronted van with a Chevy logo. With a different paint job it would have looked like Scooby Doo's Mystery Machine.

The passenger's side window rolled down and a smiling young woman waved at him. "We couldn't pass by a fellow traveler," she said.

"Thank you so much for stopping," he said, amazed at his luck.

"Jump in," she said, gesturing behind her.

He fiddled with the door handle for a second, got it open, and gratefully climbed in.

"I'm Linda, and this is my old man, Marcus," she said, nodding at the driver, who had turned back toward him.

He didn't look old enough to be her father, Mason thought, so it must be her boyfriend. He certainly had a lot of hair.

"I'm Mason."

"Hey, Mason," he said. "Have you been out here long?"

"No, actually, just half an hour or so. I'm glad you stopped before it got too hot."

"You look like you've been parboiled already," Linda said, and Marcus turned back to driving, bringing the van up to highway speed.

Mason forced a smile. "That's just being a redhead. It's … been a weird morning." He looked around on the bench seat. "No seatbelts back here?"

"No, man, no belts," Marcus said. "Are you coming from San Francisco? We were up there a few weeks ago. We've been working our way down to LA."

"Uh, no, I'm from LA." Mason settled into the middle of the seat, slightly unnerved at not being belted in.

"It's the groovy psychedelic shoes. They look very San Francisco," Linda said.

Mason looked down at his dusty orange sneakers. "OK," he said, not quite believing her. "So, are you headed directly to Los Angeles? That's where I'm hoping to get today." He took a closer look at the two of them, and wondered why they were so cheerfully accepting of finding a stranger walking down the highway in the middle of nowhere. Linda had a wild bunch of hair, some of it under the control of a blue scarf. They were both dressed casually in jeans and loud, summery cotton shirts.

"Yeah, we'll make LA today," Marcus said. "It's not far. But time, man—it's completely bogus. It doesn't mean anything."

"I'd have to say I agree with that," Mason said slowly. "But that only seems to work in metaphysical terms, as in time is a construct. I've never found that knowledge especially useful in everyday life."

"You know what they say. Free your mind," Marcus said.

"I'm with you, man," Mason said. "But I think maybe I've gone too far with it. I'm having trouble keeping reality in focus."

"Far out," Linda said emphatically, turning to look at him, clearly impressed.

"It's not actually a good thing," Mason said. "I don't even know where my phone is."

They both laughed, and Marcus said, "It sounds like you've been smoking. We should catch up." Linda fished around in a grubby backpack between the front seats, finally producing a tiny metal box. She opened it carefully and extracted a joint.

"Are you cool?" Marcus asked, looking up at Mason in the rearview mirror.

"With pot? It's fine if you want to smoke," Mason said. "I'm not going to join you, though. I need to keep a clear head."

"Suit yourself," Linda said, flipping open a Zippo lighter, sucking deeply as she lit the end of the joint. She passed it to Marcus, who expertly maintained control of the vehicle with one hand while taking long drags on it with the other. Soon the van was full of skunky-sweet haze.

Mason wondered fleetingly if their weed was strong enough for him to get high from the second-hand smoke. "Do you have a prescription for it?" he asked.

Marcus and Linda both laughed. "I wish," she said.

Mason sat in silence while they finished the joint. Secondhand pot smoke was the least of his worries, he decided. But it would be nice to eat something. He twisted around to look in the back of the van. They had clearly been on the road for a while, as it was loaded with stuff: a couple of big camping backpacks, clothes, shoes, even a stray magazine, but nothing edible. He reached back and picked up the magazine; it was an old copy of *Life,* with a very young Jackie O on the cover, in a frilly dress and standing under an umbrella.

"Some chick left that in here," Linda said, sounding spaced-out now.

"I was just talking about her last night," Mason said, twisting the cover toward Linda. "She looked great back then."

"Back then? I thought that was fairly new," Linda said.

"February 1971," Mason said, looking at the date on the cover. "You must like vintage magazines."

Linda stared at him blankly. "What are you talking about? It's from February." She laughed. "What's old is that whole type. Like, the establishment."

That must have been strong stuff, Mason thought.

Linda continued, "Why don't they put a real person on the cover, like Jane Fonda? She's out there stumping against the war."

"They put her on magazine covers back then too," Mason said.

"Back then?" Linda said, turning around to stare at Mason, her eyes narrowed. "What are you talking about?"

"You're tripping me out, man," Marcus said, and laughed.

What is going on in this van? Mason wondered. He was starting to wish he'd never gotten in. There was definitely something wrong with them. And they definitely had a 1970s theme going on, with the old van and all the hair. Even the clothes, he realized.

"Well, you can probably get some money for this thing," Mason said, tossing the magazine in the back.

"You are one strange cat," Marcus said. Linda turned back to watch the highway, and the three of them rode in silence for a while.

Soon a mountain range loomed ahead, and Mason saw an old-school road sign—LOS ANGELES: 52 MILES. That wouldn't take long. There was more traffic now, and every vehicle that went by seemed to be a vintage car. Maybe there was a classic car rally nearby that they were all headed to. The billboards were freaky out here too, and there seemed to be a lot of them, for hamburgers, soda pop, and then one that he stared at as it rolled by, for RCA COLOR TELEVISIONS. RCA? That company was ancient history.

He felt numb. What if Linda and Marcus were being serious? It would explain why Daniel's house was missing—it wouldn't have been built yet. But how could he be in a different year? He looked at the oncoming traffic, and without exception every car had either black or blue license plates, which he'd only ever seen on old cars that had been wearing them since the sixties and seventies.

He reached around and picked up the issue of *Life* again, and looked closely at the pages. It was dog-eared, but it didn't look old at all. The paper was crisp and white. He felt the cold creeping up his back again.

"Marcus," he said, leaning forward, "what did this van cost you?"

"My dad bought it," he said, sounding slightly chagrined to admit that. "It was a couple of years old and had a lot of miles on it. I think he paid eight hundred bucks."

"I see," Mason said. That was definitely a 1970s price.

"Are you shopping for a car?" Linda asked.

"No, just curious what they cost these days," Mason said, and they lapsed into silence again.

Was this really happening? All the evidence fit—the old cars, Linda and Marcus's clothes, even the absurdity of the missing house made sense in this light. Peggy would love this, he thought fleetingly, all her favorite music had been written in the seventies. Peggy! Where was she now?

He closed his eyes and worked to clear his mind, pushing away the panic that was closing in. He forced himself to focus on the here and now. How did he get here? No, more important, he thought, *why* was he here? Odd things had been happening since they had driven out to the desert, but this surpassed all the other weirdness by far. He wondered if embracing psychic power full-time, as a career choice, had overwhelmed him—he had dived in headfirst and now he didn't know which way the surface was.

This has to be happening for a reason, he told himself. Some part of his subconscious must have agreed to it. It wasn't random; it was significant, and he was participating in it willingly. Was it possible he'd made this happen? The thought was exhilarating. But the other possibility, that it was accidental, meant that it might not be reversible—he pushed that thought out of his head as quickly as it had come.

But maybe thinking it was happening for a reason was hubris. Miss Cassie had questioned whether his psychic insights were for him alone, or accessible to anyone. At the moment it seemed like he was completely alone in this, and he'd certainly gone farther into a metaphysical experience than he'd thought possible.

What choice did he have but to embrace it, let it play out? There was no other option, hubris or not. The best way to do that was to stay calm, he told himself. Rule number one was still valid—don't freak out. Next, don't jump to any conclusions. This had to be a psychic thing, something he'd asked for somehow, something he needed to figure out, and if he kept his mind open, maybe he'd get the information he was seeking. Think of it like a lucid dream, he told himself.

He took a deep breath and looked out at the road. They'd merged onto a freeway, getting closer to the city. Marcus stayed in the outside lane, slower than the rest of the traffic, his overly cautious driving probably induced by the pot. On the left a VW bus overtook them, dark red with bright yellow daises painted all over it. Marcus glanced at it but made no comment. It felt so unfamiliar.

"Don't freak out," Mason said to himself under his breath.

"Are you freaking out?" Linda asked, turning back to him, looking concerned. "Are you on acid or something?"

"No, not on acid, just a little stressed. I, uh … haven't been back to LA for quite a while. I'm not sure what to expect."

"Girl troubles?" she asked, smiling sympathetically.

"No, I'm gay," Mason said reflexively, not thinking about what that would mean in 1971.

"Whoa, man," Marcus said, looking at him in the rearview mirror. "For real, or did you just say that to get yourself out of the draft?"

"For real," Mason said, and felt his face reddening as they looked at each other, neither of them saying anything.

Finally, Linda said, "Well, I guess everybody's got their own crazy stuff."

Mason decided to let that go. What was truly crazy was that they seemed like modern people, alternative even, but they obviously had biases. It was part of their culture, part of their era, but still, it was jarring. He wondered what else he would have to worry about here. Did they still have polio in the 1970s? He'd seen photos of FDR, and polio had really messed him up. Mason tried to remember if he'd ever been vaccinated for it. Probably, a long time ago. But maybe polio was something that dated farther back, like to FDR's time. Google would know; without his phone he felt mentally hobbled. But he couldn't do much about polio or any other old-timey diseases, so focusing on that was futile. And it was easy enough to keep his mouth shut about the gay thing—that wasn't a completely unfamiliar experience even in the twenty-first century.

The freeway exit signs pointed to North Hollywood, but there were no high-rises, just rows of bungalows and low-slung strip malls. A pall of brown hung in the air, darker at the horizon. Smog, he realized. How retro was that?

They rolled through the Hollywood Hills and into the city. Marcus said, "So, Mason, can we drop you somewhere downtown?"

"Yeah, that's fine," he said. Downtown was as good a place as any. There was no point in going to his house, since he didn't live there yet.

Downtown looked completely different too, like an old photo come to life, with no office towers and way too much surface parking. Marcus got off the freeway near the Music Center; at least that looked familiar. He pulled the van over at an open patch of curb and turned back to Mason.

"Do you know how to get on the 5 from here?" he asked.

"I don't have my phone," Mason said, unlatching the door and stepping out onto the sidewalk. Neither Marcus nor Linda said anything, but they looked relieved to see him climbing out of their space. "But I think if you just get back on the freeway and head south, you'll find it."

"Well, I hope your phone is there when you get home," Linda said, concern in her eyes. She obviously thought Mason was high, or delusional, or both.

"Thanks for the ride," Mason said, and attempted a smile. Linda waved as they pulled away.

He looked around. It was good to be out of that van, but now he felt lost. The Music Center and the DWP building behind it looked the same, but other things were missing, and what was here was wrong—the giant cars, the people on the sidewalk dressed so formally. He stepped back and stood against the building that fronted the sidewalk. Most of the people walking by didn't look like Marcus and Linda; the men were wearing suits, the women dresses, and all the guys had short hair. He took a few deep breaths to still his panic. At least people were ignoring him, which meant he didn't look that out of place in his T-shirt and shorts, although a couple of passersby did a double-take when they noticed his orange sneakers.

He felt a lump in his throat, the feeling of sadness and loss. His people were gone. He was completely alone here, and had no idea even where to start. What was he supposed to do, where was he supposed to go?

Focus, he told himself. Tears weren't going to help. Focus on what's here, and now, and immediate. He needed a coffee, and food was clearly becoming a problem, as he hadn't eaten all day and it must have been close to noon; the unseen dimensions of reality hadn't made a provision for that. Getting food meant getting money, and how was he going to get his hands on that? He tried all his pockets, but there was nothing in any of them.

He was still wearing his ring, though, he realized. It was a cheap thing he'd paid maybe thirty bucks for, but it was real silver; maybe he could sell it and get some lunch. The Jewelry District was probably in the same place he knew it to be, just a few blocks away. Surely someone there would buy a piece of silver. Maybe this could work. He set off walking, relieved to have a plan.

Walking down toward First Street, ogling the parking lots where he knew there to be office buildings, theaters, and museums, he realized he was completely convinced that this was happening, that he had slipped through time. But what if he really was in some kind of lucid dream, like Miss Cassie had suggested, and he just couldn't distinguish it from reality? Or could it be a very intense and long-lasting psychometry experience, like the one he'd had with Gilbert's brooch? For that to be true, he decided, there should be some indicator that it wasn't real. He could smell food cooking, feel the sidewalk under his feet. It was too all-encompassing to be illusory. Even so, as he stopped to wait to cross the street, he closed his eyes for a moment and said under his breath, "Wake up." Everything was the same when he opened his eyes.

When he reached Sixth Street he found a jewelry store with lots of gold on display in the windows. It was worth a try. He stepped in and walked up to the counter. It was a big place, and there were several people working with customers, but before long an older man walked over to Mason, his eyes flicking down and back up, taking in Mason's clothes. He looked harried, with his slicked-back hair straying out of place, his necktie loose, and his shirtsleeves rolled up past his elbows. Still, he smiled pleasantly and said, "Can I help you?"

"I hope so. I wanted to turn this ring into some cash," Mason said, pulling it off his finger and handing it to the clerk.

"This isn't a pawn shop," he said, frowning, but he took the ring and inspected it.

"I know. But I don't need it back, and it's real silver."

"I can see that," the man said, and fished his jeweler's loupe out of his shirt pocket. As he held it up to his eye, Mason saw that he had a number tattooed on his forearm, five or six dark-blue digits in an odd stylized font.

"Groovy tattoo," he said.

The jeweler pulled the loupe from his eye and raised his eyebrows. "I have the Germans to thank for that," he said, putting the ring on the counter and folding his arms.

He was a Holocaust survivor, Mason realized. "Oh, god, I'm sorry. I didn't know ... that's not groovy at all."

"No, it's not." He looked at Mason carefully for a moment, then laughed and shook his head. "You're dressed like a punk, but it doesn't look like you're on drugs."

"I'm not," Mason said, bristling. Although, in a way, he thought, this whole day was a trip.

"I can give you four bucks for the ring, but you can't come back in here the next time you're short on cash."

"Four dollars?" Mason said, dismayed. "I bought that in Thailand. How about ten?"

"I'll give you five, right now, and then I never want to see you in here again unless you're buying."

"OK, five it is," Mason said, slightly taken aback. The jeweler pulled a wad of cash out of his pants pocket and peeled off five ones. "Thanks," Mason said, stuffing the cash into his shorts, and nodded to him before turning to leave.

Five dollars didn't sound like a lot of money, but it would go farther here than where he was from. He knew exactly where to go: the hundred-year-old central market, where fruit and veggies were as cheap as they come; it was just a couple of blocks up Broadway.

Sure enough, it looked exactly the way he knew it. Amazing how such a busy place could sail through the decades unchanged. It was calming, grounding to see that. He bought tomatoes and bread, a couple of apples, and a cluster of grapes, and laughed when he got a fistful of coins in change for a dollar bill. He bought a coffee, sadly not espresso, but at least it was strong. He sat at one of the metal tables in the market hall, where wood shavings covered the floor. It was lunchtime, and people crowded the tables with plates of tacos and Chinese food. A woman seated nearby watched Mason wide-eyed as he wolfed down his tomatoes, eating them greedily like they were apples, the juice running down his chin. She looked away quickly when he winked at her. He would have said hello, but he wasn't willing to stop eating long enough to be able to speak.

He felt so much better after ingesting some food and caffeine—almost content, almost like he could enjoy this place. Not forever, but maybe for a short psychic vacation. He stood up and stretched, smiled at the woman who had been watching him, and walked out to the street. Now what? He probably should have formulated a plan that extended beyond getting lunch, but he really was at a complete loss. There were places he could go, of course, that would be familiar, but with what goal? He walked south along the bottom edge of Bunker Hill. The city felt familiar and

unfamiliar at the same time; most strikingly, anything tall was missing, like the horizon had been
ironed flat. There seemed to be more words every-
where too, more textual advertising, more letter-
ing on street signs. Was the future less literate?

Maybe he could intuit what he was supposed
to do here, he thought, and sat down on a bus-
stop bench. If this whole thing was a psychic
experience, maybe he could get access to psychic information. He closed his eyes and tuned
out the noise of the passing traffic. He tried to
clear his mind, focusing on nothing, and asked,
"Where to?" It seemed like a simpler, more accessible question than "What am I doing here?" He
waited for something to come to mind, and then
asked again. Daniel's library came to mind, but
technically it didn't exist yet, so he ignored the
thought. The gold brooch appeared, brilliant and
timeless. Surely that couldn't be why he was here.
He opened his eyes. It didn't seem like any of this
was useful.

In the distance he noticed a pyramid with
a shiny circular logo on it. Was it a theater? he
wondered, and then it clicked: it was the central
library. He rarely saw the pyramid capping the
building because it was dwarfed by office towers all around, but now it was one of the taller
structures and he could see it from blocks away.
He loved that place; it was as logical a destination
right now as any.

He set off, looking into the restaurants and

shops along Hill Street as he walked past, marveling at the vintage clothes. Artificial fabrics in neon colors were apparently an exciting new technology. And the elaborate women's hairdos—it must have been a lot of work putting those together, even with the help of empty sardine cans, as Ned had explained. He walked by a signboard perched on the curb that read "Vegan Doughnuts," with an arrow pointing into a store. Was vegan even a thing so long ago?

He stopped and looked at the sign and the store. He knew this building, and this stretch of shops. It was an overpriced pizza joint in his day, and the grime had been sandblasted off the stone facing, but right now it was a fluorescent-lit doughnut shop. He certainly had room for a couple of vegan doughnuts, no matter how much fruit he'd eaten. He stepped into the store and looked into the case. They looked like the regular old artery-clogging doughnut variety, but another sign behind the counter said "No animal products."

There was no one at the counter, but in the back he could see a petite woman perched on a tall stool next to some kind of stainless steel doughnut-making apparatus. She was reading a folded newspaper, unaware or unconcerned that he was at the front counter. He recognized her instantly: it was Hanh, the owner of Pretty Nail Blowout, who had worked on Ned's manicure.

But it couldn't be. Was he totally racist, thinking it was the same person because she happened to be Vietnamese? But she really did look exactly like Hanh, with the same wedge haircut, awfully modern for this era. She looked up, and when she saw him her eyes narrowed.

Mason was startled—she seemed to recognize him. He had read a lot about interpreting people's reactions for one of his first cases, and what this woman's face said was "I know you." But that was impossible.

"Hi there," he called to her. "I was admiring your doughnuts."

"Of course you were," she said, scowling, and slid off the stool, walking up behind the counter and folding her arms. "Nice manicure," she said, not looking at his hands but holding his gaze.

"It *is* you," Mason said, shocked. "What are you doing here?"

"You should ask yourself the same question," she said, clearly angry now.

"I don't know what I'm doing here. I don't know how I got here," he said, his voice rising, gesturing to the street outside. "I'm standing in a vegan doughnut shop in the 1970s with Ned's manicurist. It doesn't make any sense. I'm beginning to suspect none of this is real."

Quick as lightning, Hanh swung her arm over the counter and slapped him hard across the face. "How's that for real?" she said.

Mason put his hand to his cheek. "You slapped me," he said softly, completely stunned. She was a little slip of a thing, but she packed a wallop.

"I'm glad you noticed," she said. "Remember that. All this is real, and you need to take responsibility."

"For what?" he said. "Why are you upset with me?"

She ignored his question and said, "You're broke, correct?"

"Uh … I have, like, three dollars. I sold my ring."

"Fuck, Mason," she exploded, banging her palm on the glass countertop. She looked at him for a minute. "Well, there's nothing you can do about it now." She cranked open the drawer on the retro cash register and pulled out some bills, handing them across the counter to him. "Take it," she said, when he hesitated.

"Forty-two bucks?" he said, flipping through the bills.

"That's a fortune here, you ingrate."

"I didn't mean that," he said quickly. "I just … Hanh, what's happening?"

"What's happening is that you're going to put that in your pocket. Go on, put it away."

He did as she said, stuffing the bills into his pants.

She waited until he finished and said calmly, "Now you're going to walk out of here, and you're not going to come back."

"But what—"

"No," she interrupted him, raising a finger. "I can't help you anymore. You have to sort it out yourself." She glared at him for a moment, and then said more gently, "You already know why you're here, and you're the only one with access to that information. I shouldn't even be talking to you."

"But—what are you doing here?"

"Selling doughnuts. Now, go."

He hesitated, wanting to ask her so many questions. "OK," he said, "but can I at least get a couple of these? I never see vegan doughnuts," he explained.

Hanh scowled but picked up a little paper bag and deftly flicked it open. "Which one?"

"How about a bear claw … and maybe a Boston cream? How amazing is that, vegan Boston cream." He grinned and leaned closer to the counter, momentarily forgetting about her unexplained anger and the slap, and said conspiratorially, "It's like I've time-traveled to heaven."

She slid the doughnuts into the bag and handed it across to him. "Forty cents," she said, raising her eyebrows.

Mason dug in his hip pocket for the coins, and counted them onto the countertop.

"Now, go," she said forcefully.

Mason stepped out onto the street reluctantly, clutching his bag of doughnuts. He looked back into the shop, but Hanh must have already gone into the back. He turned and started walking. Just when he'd thought things couldn't get any weirder, he'd run into someone he knew. At least she had confirmed for him, indirectly, that there was a reason for him to be here. She'd also implied that some part of him knew why he was here; that was comforting.

But what the hell was she doing here anyway, running a doughnut shop, of all things? It had to be something just for Mason, to grab his attention—something he couldn't resist, and someone he already knew. That meant he had work to do here—at last, a purpose. But he was still going to have to figure out what that was.

And why had she slapped him? His cheek still throbbed, and he was sure it was bright red. He thought about it. Maybe it was to emphasize that he wasn't dreaming, that this was still the real world. That meant he had to take responsibility, as she had said, for safely navigating this place.

He felt happy, he realized, after the encounter, and lighter, even though he'd been smacked, and it wasn't just the remarkably tasty Boston cream that was inducing that feeling. Meeting Hanh had been reassuring. She seemed to think that he could figure out what was going on, and why he was here, and that meant it might be reversible. And if she was here because he was here, it was no accident—he was here for a reason.

He came up to Fifth Street and found a broad lawn stretching out on the other side of the street, with a few scraggly ficus trees planted here and there. That certainly wasn't there in his day, he thought, but then he saw the familiar front of the Baltimore Hotel beyond the lawn. This had to be an earlier incarnation of Pershing Square. He looked around, and sure enough, there was Miss Cassie's office building, the lovely art deco tower, right where it should be off the square. He wondered where Miss Cassie was; certainly not up there. It would be nice to have one of their chats right now—she'd have a field day with this situation. He crossed the street and walked into the park, munching on his bear claw, amazed at how big the space felt compared to its claustrophobic modern version. There were signs to keep off the grass, but he wandered across it anyway, enjoying the softness under his feet, looking up at the Baltimore. There was a familiar face in there, he remembered suddenly, that he could talk to. It wouldn't take long, and it was on the way to the library.

He folded up the empty pastry bag and stuffed it into his back pocket before dashing across the street, jaywalking between the cars. He stepped in front of a big sedan that was stopped in the traffic, and when Mason glanced through the windshield, the driver, a young guy with a crew cut, seemed appalled by such brazen rule-breaking. Despite the pot-smoking and the wild fashion, these people still seemed pretty conformist.

He pulled open the door to the Baltimore's old lobby, enjoying the puff of artificially chilled air. He'd seen it many times in person, and it had to be one of the most used filming locations in town, but still, it was beautiful and dramatic every time, the Moorish arcades on either side and the gold-leaf decorative details. He breezed through the room quickly, aware that he was underdressed and not wanting to attract attention, and trotted up the swooping stairs into the main part of the hotel. He made a beeline for the bar, finding it right where it had always been.

It was open, but there was almost no one inside, logical enough considering the time of day. Apart from the bartender a lone drinker occupied one barstool. It was such a great room, grand stonework and dark wood paneling stretching up to the high ceiling. The bartender gave him the once-over as he walked up to the bar.

"We have a dress code. Jacket and tie," he said.

"There's no one in here," Mason protested. He looked at the solitary patron farther down the bar, who was watching them with mild interest. He was wearing dark overalls emblazoned with the phone company logo. "Blondie over there isn't wearing a jacket either."

"He's a working man," the bartender said.

"So overalls are OK, but I can't come in with a T-shirt?"

"It's not easy being a redhead at the Baltimore today," the blond said to the bartender.

The bartender looked down the bar at him and said, "It's not easy being a black man at the Baltimore either."

Mason looked from one to the other. Blondie

was grinning, but the bartender wasn't. Mason wasn't sure exactly what was going on. Maybe they were commiserating about something that had been said before he walked in. "You two should unionize," Mason said.

The bartender sighed and gestured to the other end of the bar. "Sit over there, in case anyone fancy comes in."

That was where Mason wanted to sit anyway, and he walked down and climbed onto a barstool. And there she was, his confidante from back in the day: a cherubic stone angel carved into a pillar in the intricate wall backing the bar. They had spent many an evening together, and he felt that he knew her well. She hadn't changed a bit.

The bartender stepped between them, putting his hands on the bar. "What'll it be?"

"Can you make a quadruple espresso?" Mason asked.

"Are you kidding me?"

"A double, then."

"This is a bar, sir. Beer and cocktails. We don't make coffee."

"OK. Let me think." He always got coffee here when he needed a place to take a break in the frenetic neighborhood, even though it really was a bar. He didn't drink very often because Ned was in recovery, but before he'd met Ned, when he was single, he'd loved coming here. It was a great place to meet lonely corporate squares from out of town, say hello to his angel friend, get a buzz on, maybe hook up, and then take the subway home. He'd always gone on weeknights, when the serious drinkers were out. In hindsight, he was lucky he hadn't become a serious drinker himself. But he was here right now, technically before he'd met Ned, so there was no harm in having a drink. "How about Glenferrick, what would a shot of that cost me?"

"I don't have the really old stuff, but the one I do have is two twenty-five."

Mason chuckled. "Bring me a double, then. Neat."

He looked down the bar, where the guy in the overalls sat with his thick fingers wrapped around a beer glass. He glanced briefly over at Mason but quickly looked away.

Mason's drink appeared, and he pulled out one of Hanh's ten-dollar bills and set it on the bar. He cocked the glass toward his angel friend and said, "Cheers, missy." He took a tiny sip. It was delightful, of course, smooth and heady, and he realized he could probably enjoy it without getting that intoxicated, right after having inhaled two greasy doughnuts. He was glad there were no windows in the bar; he already felt a twinge of guilt about drinking in the middle of the day, and broad daylight would have made it unbearable.

Conversation was always a little one-sided with the stone angel. "Do you have something to read?" he called to the bartender, who walked over a minute later with a folded newspaper, setting it on the bar beside Mason's change and giving him a look that said, "I've got better things to do."

Someone had already read the paper, and he had to unfold it a couple of times to find the front. It was the *Los Angeles Daily Bugle,* which he knew was long defunct in his day, but here it was, in his hands. The main stories were all about the minutiae of the Vietnam War, for some reason printed as "Viet Nam." That would have been big news, of course. He flipped through the paper, scanning headlines, and almost spit out a mouthful of scotch when he came across an image of a swirly piece of jewelry. Even though the ad was in grainy black-and-white newsprint, the spirals and the tiny hammered flowers were unmistakable—it was Gilbert's golden brooch. The photo was part of a quarter-page ad for *Treasures of the New Hittites,* an exhibition at the county cultural museum.

"Damn," he said, and carefully read through the ad. The exhibition artifacts were thirty-five hundred years old. Peggy had been right—the piece dated from antiquity. The caption under the photo said only "Royal pin."

This had to be the reason he was here—it was an undeniable connection between experiencing this bygone day and the research he was supposed to be doing for Gilbert. But how had the brooch gone from showpiece in an art exhibit to hiding in Daniel's barn?

The paper was dated the 12th, and the exhibit

didn't open until the 28th, so it must have been a major event, promoted so prominently that far ahead. He paged through the rest of the paper, but there wasn't anything else about it except the ad.

"Excuse me," he called to the bartender, "Is this today's paper?"

The man looked over from his spot behind the bar, and said, "How should I know? Don't they print the date on them anymore?"

"What's today's date, is what I'm asking," Mason said.

"The 14th."

That meant he couldn't go see the exhibition yet, but maybe there would be something else written about it in a newer newspaper. How frustrating that everything was printed on paper, and he couldn't just search a website for it. How had people managed?

"I've got today's paper, Red," said the blond at the other end of the bar. He picked it up and waved it at Mason.

"Thanks, man," Mason said, sliding off his barstool and walking over, grateful for the offer. He realized being called that nickname didn't annoy him the way it would have in the past, when he'd been trapped in an office.

"Help yourself," the blond said, sliding the paper along the bar top. "Lester," he said to the bartender, "bring the man's drink over here, will you?"

Mason assessed the guy. He didn't seem drunk, despite the nearly empty pint glass in front of him. He looked a little gloomy, which probably meant he wouldn't be a chatterbox, so Mason tacitly accepted and climbed up on the adjacent barstool, folding open the newspaper. It was the *Bugle,* dated the 14th as promised. He pulled the paper aside as the bartender set his tumbler and his change down in front of him, again with a pointed look; he had told Mason to remain inconspicuous at the far end of the bar, he remembered.

"Those are quite the shoes," the blond said, looking down at his feet.

"Thank you," Mason said firmly, locking eyes with him for a moment, and then went back to the paper.

"You know, you can't get too upset with Lester."

Mason looked up. "The bartender? I wasn't upset with him."

"He has to put on a happy face for those corporate dumbbells who come in here after 5. Right now is his downtime."

Mason nodded and went back to the paper. More news about the war in the big headlines, but when he flipped the paper over, below the fold a smaller headline read "Antiquities Stolen from Museum Trucks." This had to be about the exhibition.

"I'm Danny," his new companion said, extending a meaty hand.

Mason sighed. He was dying to read the article.

"Mason," he said, setting down the paper to shake hands, then picking up his tumbler.

"You're not from around here, are you," Danny said.

"Not really. But I used to come in here, to pick up those corporate suits you were talking about." Almost before he'd finished saying it, he remembered Marcus and Linda's reaction to the gay thing, and winced, wishing he'd censored himself.

"Oh, so you're a friend of Dorothy," Danny said, looking surprised.

"Uh, yeah, I guess that's right," Mason said, wary. He knew it was an old euphemism for being gay, but he wasn't sure how Danny felt about it.

"Me too," Danny said. "But I'd never come in here to pick up guys. There are better places."

"Wow. I wouldn't have pegged you as gay," Mason said, looking at him more carefully.

"I've heard that before, brother. But we can't all be the white-pants type."

"No, I suppose not," Mason said, though he had no idea what he meant.

"You really came in here to pick up guys?" Danny asked.

"Not recently. It was a once-in-a-while kind of thing. Like when you get a hankering for Ethiopian food, so you cycle halfway across town to get lunch."

Danny frowned. Clearly he'd never had that experience. "Well, just be careful. Some of these clowns might just punch your teeth in."

"Ouch. Does that really happen?"

"You bet it does. The cops won't help you either."

That was a dismaying thought. No wonder Danny seemed glum. "So do you have a partner?" Mason asked, angling to change the subject.

"You mean a lover? No," he said, and smiled. "I got close once, but he got shipped off to the war."

"I thought there was a gay exemption, that you could get out of the draft if you came out to them."

"If they believe you. But who would tell them that? I'd lose my job."

"Damn," Mason said, shaking his head. "Well, here's to rapid social evolution." He clinked his tumbler on Danny's beer glass.

"Cheers," Danny said, taking a swig, but he looked confused. "So are you looking for work?"

"What?"

"The newspaper," he said, gesturing to the *Daily Bugle* on the bar.

"Oh, no. I was just reading about this exhibition, *Treasures of the Early Hittites.*"

"*Treasures of the New Hittites,*" Danny corrected him. "That burglary has been all over the radio today."

"Really? What are they saying about it?"

"Well," Danny said, leaning toward Mason, "it's a great story. There's all this ancient art and artifacts headed for the exhibition, and it's coming from the airport on moving trucks, and some of it doesn't get to the museum. What's in the crates doesn't match the manifest. The museum people say maybe the Turks didn't ship everything that they said they did, and the Turks say it must have gone missing on this end. Or maybe someone broke into the boxes on the airplane when it landed in Frankfurt, or in New York. The cops are saying they think it was a burglary from one of the trucks, here in LA."

Moving trucks, Mason thought—there's the connection. Gilbert's dad had run a moving company. That had to be it; maybe Daniel had stolen the brooch when he'd been moving it. Why else would it have been hidden so carefully?

"How much stuff went missing?" Mason asked.

"Just a few pieces, but they were priceless because they're so old. I'd hate to be that museum's insurance guy right now."

Mason nodded.

Danny swallowed the last of his beer. "I've got to get back to work. Listen, Mason, do you need some cash? You look like you're a little down on your luck."

"Do I?" Mason said. He knew he was underdressed for this place, but he hoped he didn't look like he'd wandered over from Skid Row. "No, brother, but thanks. I appreciate the offer."

"Well, maybe I'll see you out in town. There's a great club in Pedro that I go to, real nice people, no jacket required." He stepped off his barstool and gave Mason a crooked grin.

"Yeah, maybe I'll see you out there," Mason said. "Thanks." You never knew what people were all about at first glance, Mason thought, watching him walk out.

He turned back to the newspaper and read quickly through the article about the museum truck. It was essentially what Danny had told him: the police hadn't said why they thought the theft had happened on the truck, but that was the theory that they were working from. He tore out the article, carefully ripping the paper around its edges. He did the same with the ad that had the image of Gilbert's brooch from the older newspaper, then folded both clippings together and slid them into his rear pocket.

The bartender stood not far away, concern in his eyes, watching Mason ripping up the newspaper.

"Well, Lester, it's just you and me now," Mason said.

"I see that."

"But sadly, my friend, I'm going to have to take my leave as well." He drained his tumbler in one gulp. It burned his throat, and he felt slightly guilty for wasting good scotch that way. "I heard you've got the fancy guys coming in here soon, so I'm going to leave you three of these singles as an expression of my condolences."

"Hey, thanks," Lester said, genuinely grateful.

Mason nodded to him, then picked up the rest of his change and stuffed it in his pants as he headed out into the hotel's grand hallway. He was a little buzzed, he realized, but also excited about possibly having solved the mystery of the brooch. But at the same time, it felt too easy. Could that really be the reason he was here? He could have found that newspaper article in the library when they got back to the city. He didn't need to be here at the scene of the crime, in person, getting slapped around by doughnut jockeys and drinking scotch with blue-collar blonds. There had to be more to it.

He stepped out onto the sidewalk and walked toward the end of the block. He still intended to go to the library, but across the street the lawn in Pershing Square looked inviting. Some young people were sitting on the grass, despite the posted prohibition; maybe he could just lie there too for a few minutes. It had been a long day.

Walking along the construction fence that lined the sidewalk, he noticed with a start that the poster on one of the plywood panels was for Treasures of the New Hittites, complete with a full-color image of Gilbert's golden brooch. He laughed, and then saw the same poster a few feet farther along. "Not subtle," he said aloud. "Not subtle at all." He laughed harder as they tripled, and then quadrupled, and after passing the sixth or eighth one he leaned against the fence and doubled over with laughter, hardly able to breathe. The entire length of the fence was plastered with the brooch.

A woman passed him on the sidewalk, watching him, wide-eyed and frowning, and clutched her handbag to her chest. Time to move along, Mason thought, wiping his eyes, his mirth subsiding. His father had said you can be as eccentric as you want until you start scaring people. The last thing he needed was to get arrested because they thought he was on LSD, and thrown in the clink, where he'd probably catch polio.

It was so silly, so in-your-face, to find thirty copies of the mysterious brooch posted right in front of him. Was this really how reality was going to work, at this level of absurdity, now that he'd signed up for full-on psychic experiences?

Maybe the posters appeared to remind him of why he was here, to emphasize what he'd read in the paper. Or maybe as a duplication, in case he'd missed the newspaper article. If some part of him was generating this experience, that was exactly something he would do: build in duplicates, reminders, safeguards. Still, it was hard to accept that he'd created this whole loopy place.

It put things in perspective, that was for sure. Miss Cassie talked a lot about emotional states, nudging him to try to figure out how they overlapped and fed into one another. The anger he'd felt on Friday about being left out of Pretty Nail

Blowout seemed ridiculous in light of what was happening today. He'd been exhilarated by the emotional release of smashing up pottery with Gilbert, but it paled in comparison to finding thirty copies of the brooch, confronting him again and again with a precise answer to the question Gilbert had asked him—its provenance. He admired the posters one last time, shaking his head.

He walked across the street and into the park, scanning the area for the uniforms of police or security guards, and then flopped down onto his back. It was cool and soft, so easy to get comfortable on, but he decided not to take off his shoes. He put his arm across his eyes to block the bright sun. Just a few minutes, he told himself. He might not even fall asleep.

"Excuse me, sir. The sign says 'Keep off the grass.'"

Mason started awake, squinting into the blinding brightness at an indistinct blob hovering over him. He couldn't see the face, but after he blinked a couple of times, he recognized the brittle black hair. "Laura?"

"I'm just messing with you. I'm not the cops," she said, and grinned at him. "I knew you'd head for LA, but I thought I might be able to beat you here."

Mason sat up. "What are you doing here?"

"I could ask you the same question."

"Don't start with me," he said, irritated. He looked around, feeling disoriented, but he could see he was still on the broad green lawn.

"You have to come with me."

"Oh, yeah, OK," he said, nodding facetiously. "Guess what's not going to happen? Back off, sister, I'm trying to take a nap here."

Laura laughed and put her hands on her hips. "What exactly do you think is going on?"

"I think you may have had something to do with me getting stuck in this fun house, so I'm not going to follow you anywhere. You're trouble."

"Don't you think I might be able to help you get out of here?"

"OK," Mason said, rubbing his eyes. "But you're such a strange person." He stood up and met her eye. "I think I'm having trust issues."

"I am a strange person," she said simply. "And I understand why you wouldn't trust me. I wasn't really focused when we met … before. But I can probably answer some of your questions. You have a few, don't you?"

"Yeah."

"There's a diner over there on the corner, see? Let me buy you a sandwich."

"I'm full up on vegan doughnuts and scotch," Mason said, "but you could buy me a coffee."

As they walked toward the diner, Mason took a good look at her. She was dressed like a desert rat again, in plaid and denim, but she seemed more present, more normal. And her lips were thin, but they were there; Peggy had been wrong about them disappearing completely.

She glanced over at him and grinned.

"What's so funny?" he asked.

"I'm glad you fell asleep in the park."

"Why is that?"

"It's how I found you. Your brain generates theta waves when you sleep. Everyone's does. It lit up like a bonfire."

"Really," Mason said, confused but intrigued.

At the diner, Laura pulled open the door for Mason to step inside. He caught the eye of the waitress at the counter and gestured at an empty booth by the window. She nodded, and Mason slipped onto the bench seat. Laura sat across from him.

"Coffee, black," he said when the waitress came over.

Laura said, "For me too. And do you have pie? I'd love a nice slice of apple pie."

"Do you want that warmed up, honey?" the waitress asked.

"It doesn't matter. She's not going to eat it," Mason said.

"Yeah, warm it up," Laura told her, and then to Mason, "You're acting awfully prickly for someone whose neck I'm going to save."

"Is that what's happening?"

"Yes, Mason," she said emphatically, leaning toward him.

"You seem like a real person now," he said. "At dinner last night you were so distracted, almost robotic." He thought for a moment. "Please tell me you're not a robot."

She laughed, and waited as the waitress set down two coffee cups. "I'm definitely not a robot."

"But you don't even know who Jackie O was."

"I could find out who he was if I needed that information, but that's not important right now. I'm here to sort things out." She took a sip of her coffee.

"Finally, the woman drinks," Mason said, rapping on the table with his knuckles. "I thought maybe you lived on air and sunlight alone."

"There was a lot going on when I saw you yesterday. I was parallel processing. I'm a bit like you, Mason, in that I know there's more going on in the world than what you can see and touch. I was busy in another part of reality yesterday, so the part of me that you saw seemed unfocused."

Mason stared at her. No one in his life shared his understanding of how things really worked. This was important. "So you're saying you're some kind of multidimensional person? You're here but you have doppelgängers in other versions of reality?"

"Not doppelgängers. It's still me. And not other versions, just other ..." She didn't seem to be able to find the word. "Do you know how time zones work?"

"Generally, sure," Mason said, and sipped his coffee.

"So as an example, if it's Tuesday here and Friday in another place, part of me can be working here, and part of me is working there."

"That's not how time zones work," Mason said slowly.

The waitress set a plate with a slice of pie on it in front of Laura, who picked up her fork and dug into it with gusto, savoring the first bite.

"It's really good," she said, her mouth half full of pie. "You should have some."

"No thanks." He watched her eat, and when she showed no sign of slowing down, he said, "I still don't understand."

"OK." She set her fork down and used her hands to illustrate her words. "When you pull up a Web page, the screen is in the room with you, right, but the content is stored on other machines. The text might be here in California, the photos in Asia, and the little advertisements are in Europe. It's like me—my body is here, but what I'm thinking and saying is stored elsewhere. Sometimes the pages load quickly, and sometimes there's a delay."

"Kind of like the dream world?" Mason asked. "I'm there when I'm dreaming, but I'm also here."

She took another bite of pie and nodded.

"What I really want to know, though, is what I'm doing here, in the wrong time."

"You're psychic, right?"

"That's what it says on my business card," he said. "Seriously, though, yes. I don't have as much control of it as I'd like, not yet, but yes."

"So, as a psychic, you're open to information that crosses over from other parts of reality, right?

You have your lucid dreams, and your psychometry, and you get information that way. You also get information in the form of inspiration, and you don't know where that comes from."

"Yes, that's all true." How did she know all that about him?

"So all this"—she waved her fork at the diner—"is like a very lucid dream. It's so lucid that you slipped right from there"—she tapped her fork on the napkin dispenser—"to here"—her coffee cup. "Or more precisely, from then to now."

"And what caused that?" He spoke intently. "Is this going to happen all the time? Is it like I put my feet in the psychic swimming pool and then I fell to the bottom of the deep end? And did you have something to do with it?"

"You already know that," she said.

"Not really."

"Think about it," she said. "Use your intuition, and tell me how you got here."

She really does know how all this psychic insight stuff works, he thought. He tried to clear his mind, watching her eat rather than closing his eyes as he usually did. He knew the answer, he realized, but he didn't know how he knew. It might be little more than a guess, but more likely it had come from somewhere—as she had said, inspiration.

"I walked out to your campsite last night," he said finally. "There was something going on there, a humming sound, and a blue light. I don't know what that was, but somehow it was a doorway or a catalyst or something that made me slip into the past."

"Yes," she said, setting down her fork. "Well done."

"But was it intentional? Did you kick me in the pants to send me through time, or was it an accident?"

"Again, you know the answer to that," she said. "Go on, think about it."

He took a swig of coffee, and anticipated the information. He was figuring out how to be receptive, to open his mind, he realized, and he was getting better at it, because it was getting easier. It was like stargazing. If you looked directly at a star in the sky at night, it would disappear, but if you looked slightly away from it, not focusing on it, it became clearly visible. Not focusing on the information he wanted, but letting it drift in on its own, seemed to work that way too.

"It wasn't intentional," he said. "Whatever you were doing affected me, caused me to shift, but you didn't plan that."

"A gold star for Mason," she said.

"But what is it that you were doing? And how did you know where I'd gone?"

She sighed. "Those things are hard to explain."

"Try," Mason said, but wondered if she would be able to, based on her confusing time zone analogy.

"I went to that arroyo because there are

distortions there," she began.

He nodded encouragement and wrapped both hands around his coffee cup.

"I went to resolve the distortions."

"Distortions in what?" he asked, his eyes narrowing.

"Distortions in everything. The structure of reality, the flow of time. Not big distortions, just disturbances, really. I was trying to find out what was wrong."

"I didn't notice anything distorted when I was there," he said.

"But Daniel did, and Gilbert was aware of it too. They were there more."

"Gilbert said he saw lights in the sky. Is it that kind of thing?"

"That's part of it," she said. "Do you know how cable TV works?"

He sighed. "I know how my remote control works."

"Sometimes the cable breaks down in your neighborhood, though, doesn't it? You get channel 2, your neighbor gets channel 3, someone down the street gets 2 and 3 superimposed, someone else just gets the test pattern with the guy in the feather headdress, and in another house the cable catches fire and burns up."

"OK, that never happens."

"But you get the idea: the cable signal can get distortions or disruptions in it. The structure of reality works the same way."

"So what was causing the distortion?"

"It's not time to talk about that yet," she said, and smiled.

"Oh, my god, woman, come on," he said.

"I'm not denying you the information," she said. "I just haven't compiled that information yet."

It was an awkward way to phrase it, but he believed her. So she was a cosmic repair woman, mending reality like Danny back at the Baltimore fixed phone lines. Maybe she wasn't a robot, but with a job like that she wasn't an ordinary person either. He had a sudden thought. "Laura," he said slowly, "can I ask you a personal question?"

"Of course."

"Are you an alien?"

"No," she laughed. "I'm a person, just like you."

"Born on this planet? Can you show me some ID?"

"Mason, I'm as human as you are. We're a lot alike, even though you probably don't see that. You're dipping your toe in the surf along the shore, and I'm way out there swimming with the cuttlefish, but it's the same ocean."

"It makes me wonder about the whole time-slip thing. Your work, or research, or whatever it was you were doing, is what caused it, but I was somehow complicit, or gave my assent, right?"

"Once again," she said, and raised her eyebrows.

"I already know the answer. Right, right." He

thought for a moment. He did know the answer, but he wasn't entirely sure whether from psychic insight or just ordinary deductive reasoning. "I must have been down with it, because it happened," he said. "Some part of me either made this happen or is complicit in it. And I landed here specifically because there was information here to help me solve the case I'm working on. It was so blatant that it made me crack up laughing in the middle of the street. Somehow I chose this time."

"That sounds right," she said. "It's your lucid dream, so you set up the parameters."

"And hey," he said, remembering, "do you know Hanh, this woman who runs a nail salon, and I think maybe also a vegan doughnut shop?"

"Of course. She's one of us."

"What do you mean?"

"She's like you and me. She's able to project herself, or lucid dream, to the point that she's actually here too, like we are."

"Why was she so upset with me today? She slapped me right across the face."

"Imagine you're in a restaurant, and everyone is sitting around eating and chatting."

She certainly loves analogies, Mason thought, folding his arms.

"And then a child walks in, a toddler who's never been to a restaurant before, and doesn't know the conventions of a restaurant or how to behave, not even how to get food. This kid walks around and breaks the legs off tables, and flips people's plates over, and smashes holes in the floor."

"I don't know many toddlers who could do that," Mason said, frowning.

"But you get the idea. When someone doesn't know how things work, they can cause a lot of damage."

"Of course. Is that me?"

"You've never done this before. Hanh was justifiably concerned that you conduct yourself appropriately. She didn't want you to break any table legs or flip any plates over."

"Have I done something wrong?"

"You shouldn't have sold your ring. But you didn't know that, and you won't do it again."

"How do you know about that?"

"You told me all about it," she said, waving her hand to brush the matter away.

Laura had a strange ability to figuratively see around corners, but even more curious was the idea that Mason could willingly immerse himself in another time. "You're implying that I could come back here again, like Hanh," he said.

"You can."

It was an exciting idea, and it meant he was actually getting somewhere with this career, sharpening his skills.

"So why doesn't Hanh just buy a whole bunch of shares on the stock market here, in computer companies or something that she knows will boom, and then enjoy the spoils back home, instead of running a nail salon? Why couldn't I do that while I'm here?"

"Because that would be the equivalent of punching holes in the restaurant floor," she said. "But you already knew that. And do you really think she's just running a nail salon? You have to look deeper, Mason. There's a lot more going on than what you see at first glance."

He'd had the very same insight earlier about Danny, he remembered.

"It's not a coincidence that you met Hanh in your base-now right before you came to here-now, either. If you disconnect your experiences from linear time, they make sense in a different way."

He sat quietly, absorbing it all, while she finished her pie. It was validating to have been included—"like you and me," she'd said. It meant he was capable of it, he was actually doing it, and he was being taken seriously. But at the same time it was intimidating; would he ever be able to stroll through this kind of experience as confidently and calmly as Laura, sitting there eating pie?

"I don't get one thing," Mason said. "If this is a lucid dream, why can't I just wake up? I tried to. And don't tell me to intuit the answer."

"It is a lucid dream, but it's also reality. It's both. You're really here, Mason. And a part of you that's more cautious is protecting you by not letting you just snap out of it."

"I'm pretty cautious," Mason said doubtfully.

"Well, you wound up here, which could be

construed as reckless. Hanh certainly thought so; she came here to support you. And you will wake up out of it. But to do that, I have to take you back."

"So we're going back to Natron."

"Yes. And I think you'll feel a little more rational once we get there."

"I think I'm pretty rational now."

"Seriously?" She looked at him for a moment. "You wanted me to leave you alone so you could go back to sleep on the grass out there. A rational person would have jumped for joy at the sight of a familiar face."

"I guess you're right. I wish I had a pen and paper so I could write all this down. I've learned so much today."

"*It won't persist,*" she said.

"What?"

"Listen, are you almost done with your coffee?" she said, ignoring his question. "We need to get rolling soon." She tilted her forearm and glanced at her bare wrist.

"You know that you're not wearing a watch, right?" Mason asked.

She tapped her wrist anyway, slid out of the booth, and walked toward the door.

She must have forgotten that she was buying. Mason turned to the counter and caught the waitress's eye, and mimed writing with a pen.

"One ninety," she called to him.

He grinned at the bargain and found three

singles among the bills in his pocket, setting them under his coffee cup before following Laura out of the diner.

"I'm parked over there," she said, gesturing toward the far side of the square.

They walked in silence for a few moments, and then Mason asked, "At dinner last night, did you pick up that Gilbert has a crush on you?"

"I'm aware. It's my fault, in a way. I needed to spend time there, near Daniel's house, and leading him on made it easier for me to gain access."

"He said you were rude to him in a diner. You acted like you didn't know him."

"I didn't," she said. "I wasn't in the same sequence. I was in a different time zone, like I explained earlier."

"So you actually experience things in a different time sequence than the rest of us? Doesn't that get confusing?"

"Sometimes," she admitted. "But you're very out of sequence right now too. You could go buy those computer stocks you mentioned, or visit your mother when she was a young woman."

"Why didn't I think of that?" Mason said. "I know where she lives. Can we do that?"

"You know the answer. It's like smashing holes in the restaurant floor. It's not worth it."

"It's such a great idea, though."

"No, it's not. Think about it for a minute," she said, looking him in the eye.

"OK, I get it," he said. "No visiting people."

"And about your friend Gilbert—I'll take care of it. All he sees now is the glamour—the sexy curves, the lipstick."

Mason eyed her burned-straw hair and the lumberjack blouse hanging off her shoulders like a flour sack.

"Once he sees me a little more, he'll get over it. In any case, it's not your concern."

"Fair enough," Mason said. "But he's my friend, and I think he's vulnerable right now, losing his dad. Just don't hurt him."

"Here we are," she said, clearly done discussing Gilbert. Her blue Suburban, looking old and battered even in this era, waited at the curb, hitched to the gleaming Airstream, incongruously without a dent or scratch.

"You're going to have to ride in the trailer," she said.

"Totally illegal, but I guess I trust your judgment," he said.

"I'm glad to hear it," she said, laughing. And more seriously, "I'll need to take the cash you acquired."

He pulled the bills and coins out of his pocket and handed them to her.

"Why?" he asked.

"When you visit a national park, you don't chop down trees and take them home with you, do you?"

"No." It wasn't much of an explanation, but he got the idea.

"Did you acquire anything else while you were here?"

"No," he said, "just five dollars from the ring and the forty-two that Hanh gave me."

She opened the door to the Airstream and gestured for him to get in. "Make yourself comfortable," she said. "We'll be there in a couple of hours."

Mason stepped in, apprehensive but happy to be going home. The windows were shuttered, so it was dim inside when she closed the door behind him. As his eyes adjusted to the low light he looked around the interior. At first blush it looked like a standard-issue RV. The vehicle swayed as Laura pulled away from the curb, but Mason braced himself against the wall.

The bed looks odd, he thought, walking over to it. It was the width, he decided—the size of a single bed rather than a double. It also tapered slightly, wider at one end than the other. Who would build that into a camping trailer? The wallpaper was incongruous too, he noticed, an indigo-blue and white repeating pattern of an architectural drawing. Freedom Hall in Philadelphia, maybe, or a similar building. It seemed more appropriate for a set of china than for wallpaper. He brushed his knuckles against it and found the blue parts were velvety. No way was that standard-issue either.

There didn't seem to be any personal stuff, not even clothes. Maybe she kept them in the closet and the built-in drawers. He looked at the drawer faces—there was something strange about them too. After a moment he realized that each of the drawer-pulls was a slightly different size; just a quarter of an inch at most, but all five of them were different sizes, and they didn't line up vertically. How hard was it to go to a hardware store and buy five matching handles, and then install them in a straight line? He looked at the overall effect. It snagged his gaze, like noticing that someone had two different-colored socks on. He forced himself to look away.

Overall the whole interior was just off, he decided, as if whoever had decorated it had been daydreaming. Sitting on the counter beside the tiny cooktop was an antique rotary dial phone. He smiled at the absurdity of it, a landline in a moving vehicle. Maybe Laura had a sense of humor. Mason had only ever seen them in thrift stores, but this one looked new. He picked up the handset to feel its old-school heft, put it up to his ear, and was shocked to hear a dial tone. He set it down quickly and stepped back. But why should he be surprised, after everything that had happened today?

He sat down on the bed. The vehicle seemed to be moving faster now; maybe Laura had pulled onto the freeway. The bed felt comfortable, despite its inexplicable design, and surprisingly he found he could stretch out to his full height on it. He was exhausted, he realized.

Even though he was just starting to trust

Laura, she had a plan for getting him back to Ned and Peggy and Gilbert, and he was grateful. Ned had talked about letting go of things as part of his sobriety, to stop worrying or obsessing. That sounded useful right now, just letting her do it. He couldn't really understand what Laura was talking about when she explained what she was doing, but he recognized familiar fundamental truths in the way she explained it. And regardless of whether he trusted her or not, it was all up to her now.

What had she said, just before they left the diner? It won't persist. Did that mean he wasn't going to remember this? Was that because the experience was happening in dreamland, as she had implied? He was always able to remember vivid lucid dreams, although the more prosaic dreams sometimes faded. He needed to find a way not to lose it. "Don't forget," he said aloud. "Don't let go of this. It's important."

It would be easy to fall asleep here, he thought, looking at the ceiling above Laura's bed. If they were driving all the way back to Natron, it would be hours, so he might as well sleep. Almost as soon as he'd made that decision, he drifted off.

Sunday

MASON WOKE TO THE sun in his eyes. He was still out on the arroyo, the sun just above the horizon, casting brilliant pinks and purples around the rim of the sky. He rolled onto his knees and brushed the gravelly sand off his arms. Laura's rig was long gone. He'd fallen asleep out here, and hadn't even heard her leave. How stupid, to walk all the way out here and then fall asleep. But is that what had happened? He couldn't quite remember walking up to Laura's rig last night. In any case, he hadn't gained any insight into the noise that had woken him. Maybe it had been an earthquake after all.

He stood up, brushing the sand off his knees, stretched, and set off toward the house. He could just see it from here, an indistinct box on the horizon. It was an easy walk back in daylight, and the house was quiet when he came up to it. He gently slid the patio door open, and walked to the master bedroom. Ned was still asleep. He looked at the clock on his phone. 6:08 a.m.—he'd only been out there a few hours. He slipped off his shoes and shed his clothes, crawling in beside Ned and folding his arm over his chest.

"Where were you?" Ned asked, still half asleep, turning toward him but not opening his eyes.

"I went for a walk," Mason said. It wasn't a lie, really, just a minor omission. He wasn't about to tell Ned that he'd gone exploring and had fallen asleep in the desert.

"That doesn't sound like my Mason, getting up so early," he said, and went back to sleep.

Mason wanted to sleep too, but he felt amped up. Why wasn't he tired? He couldn't have slept for more than a couple of hours out there. He cleared his mind and told himself to fall asleep, but to remember his dreams.

He was still mostly conscious when the face of the stone angel bubbled up, a sharp vision in his mind. It took him a minute to place her. The Baltimore, he remembered sleepily. But that was far from here.

"Are you OK?" Ned asked him, sitting up in the bed.

"Why do you say that?"

"Well, your eyes are open, and it's barely mid-morning."

"Funny."

Ned climbed out of bed and pulled on a T-shirt and boxer shorts. "I'm going to shower, and then see if Gilbert's up yet."

It was odd to be awake and alert so early in the day. He lay there for a while, waiting for his body to tell him to go back to sleep, but it didn't happen. He wasn't convinced it was a good idea to be up so early—he had a bit of a headache, probably from his late-night ramble—but he rolled out of bed and got dressed.

He found Ned in the kitchen flipping pancakes on the stove, Gilbert sitting at the kitchen table.

"You're up," Gilbert said, surprised.

"I'll take him to a neurologist as soon as we get back to town," Ned said, and to Mason, "How many pancakes?"

"Maybe three?" Mason said, pouring himself a coffee. "I can't believe you're making those—how cool is that." He sat at the table across from Gilbert. "Where's Peggy?"

"She ate with me a few minutes ago," Ned said. "She's back in the music room."

Mason looked across at Gilbert, whose hair was sticking up on one side from sleeping on the pomade he'd put in it the night before. Gilbert—there was something he had to tell him. It must have been something from a dream, because he couldn't quite remember what it was. He hadn't written anything down overnight. Maybe if he stopped focusing on it, it would come back on its own.

Ned set a steaming plate of pancakes down in front of each of them, then grabbed his coffee mug and sat down with them.

"These are beautiful," Gilbert said, drowning his plate in syrup.

Mason reached for the syrup bottle and asked, "How is the estate stuff going?"

"Good, I think," Gilbert said. "Nedly is figuring it out. My dad had more money than I thought."

"Assets," Ned corrected him. "It's not all cash."

"Right," Gilbert said. "It means I can relax a little and catch my breath before I have to go job hunting. We can keep this place too, if my family wants to do that, because it's paid for, and the taxes are cheap. And I won't be so tempted to sell that hunk of gold jewelry."

"Yeah, I wouldn't do that," Mason said. "Let me find out what it is first. I've got some ideas about that to work on today."

"It also means I'll be able to pay you for your research time."

"Not that there was any doubt about that," Mason said.

After breakfast Mason grabbed his laptop and writing pad and shut himself in the library. He went to the shelf with the brooch, and picked it up to admire it. The royal pin, he thought. The words appeared fully formed in his head, but he had no idea how, or from where. The angry woman he'd seen in his psychometric vision might have been royal. But Mason knew it wasn't a guess—he was certain that the brooch denoted royalty.

He sat in one of the wing chairs and set the brooch on its arm. Pulling his phone out of his pants, he found the number for the LA central library's history department and dialed.

"History," a man's voice answered, pronouncing it with just two syllables, "*hiss-tree.*"

"Is Harmony available?" Mason asked him. He'd befriended Harmony one day when she'd gone out of her way to dig up some resources he'd needed.

"One moment."

A familiar Caribbean lilt came on the line. "This is Harmony."

"Mason Braithwaite. How's my favorite librarian?"

"They must be cleaning up Skid Row again, because there's half a dozen homeless people perfuming up my area today."

"That sounds awful."

"It's not that bad. We just turn up the air-conditioning."

"Well, I won't keep you for too long—"

"Oh, I'm in no rush to get back over there," she said. "I know you wouldn't be calling me if you didn't want something, so spill it. What can I do for you?"

"You're very intuitive. I was actually thinking that you have some lovely databases over there."

"Which you can't use unless you come in to the library. We're open until 5."

"Yeah, that's where the favor part comes in. I'm not actually in town."

"And you want me to set you up with a log-in so that you can access them. That's completely against the rules."

"But not illegal, right? You didn't say the word *illegal*."

"No, but I could get in trouble. Those subscriptions cost a fortune."

"Worst-case scenario? Someone questions you about it, so you tell them one of those homeless people looked over your shoulder and copied down your log-in credentials."

"I guess," she said. "But what's in it for me, Mason?"

"The warm feeling you get from doing a good deed for your fellow man."

"Warm feelings don't pay my phone bill."

"OK, well, I'm not going to be so crass as to offer you money." He thought for a moment. "Are you still single?"

"Extremely," she said.

"I know this guy that I could introduce you to. He's been single for a while as well. I could set you up on a blind date."

"What's wrong with him?"

"Nothing. He's a great guy. He and I were

playing baseball just yesterday."

"Was it some kind of gay baseball thing? I'm not going to date a guy who dates guys. There's no way I can compete with that."

"He's straight, Harmony. He's even a bit of a ladies' man."

"So he's a man-whore. Strike one. What does he do?"

"Well, he's in a career transition right now, but he's quite busy sorting out his late father's estate."

"So he's unemployed. That's strike two. What else? Does he have a car?"

"What kind of criterion is that to decide whether you'll go on a date with someone?" Mason said. "I don't have a car, and I'm highly functional. But yes, he has a car. And he's very nice. Sensitive and thoughtful. He spiffs up nicely too; he wore a collared shirt to dinner last night."

"OK, why not—set it up. You know my number." He heard her laugh. "You ready for this info?"

Mason grabbed his yellow notepad and flipped to a blank sheet, writing down the log-in details as Harmony recited them. He hung up, and a few minutes later was connected to the newspaper and journal archive. Dozens of papers were fully indexed back to the early 1990s; before that the records became spotty, with some journals and issues digitized and others available only on microfilm in the library. He didn't have a time frame to search, but hopefully something would lead him to a news item about the brooch.

He flipped to a clean page in his notepad so that he could sort out his thoughts.

The Brooch
- has value: gold, antique
- hidden, therefore maybe stolen (newsworthy?)
- among Daniel's stuff
- Daniel from LA, ergo stolen in LA?

It was a good starting point. He searched the archive for "stolen jewelry," and then "stolen antiquities." Based on the volume of news items in the results, a lot of stuff had been stolen in that town over the years.

What was the phrase that had popped into his mind earlier? He did a search using "royal pin," and soon found an item from 1971 in the *Los Angeles Daily Bugle:* "Exhibit Continues with Recovered Jewelry." He read through it quickly. The art exhibit *Treasures of the New Hittites* had been burgled before it even opened. Some of the pieces had been recovered and mailed anonymously to the museum, but the royal pin was still missing. There was no picture of it, but the details fit—it could be Gilbert's piece. He saved a copy of the article and searched for *Treasures of the New Hittites.* There were a dozen articles, all of them dealing with the theft. He clicked on one titled "Antiquities Stolen from Museum Trucks." Why was that so damn familiar? He closed his eyes for a minute and focused on the words. *The New Hittites.*

He picked up his notepad again and flipped to the first sheet, the one he'd used at Miss Cassie's office. One of the things he'd written down that day was "Do I have access to hidden parts of reality?" He focused on that idea for a minute. It brought something up from his subconscious. He remembered sitting in a bar. The taste of scotch, someone telling him the same story about the museum trucks. He'd said *the Early Hittites,* "but the guy had corrected him, *"the New Hittites."* It bubbled up gradually, more details coming into focus. It was a struggle to dredge it up, but it felt very real. A blond guy, drinking beer, with thick, ruddy hands. And a newspaper article; he'd torn it out and shoved it into his back pocket.

Heartbeat accelerating, he reached down and felt his back pocket, but there was nothing in it. He stared at the rows of books for a minute. It's close, he thought. I've almost got it. These pants—he'd just put them on this morning, after he'd woken up the second time, after he'd gone back to sleep. These weren't the pants he'd been wearing when he went on his walk.

He stood up abruptly and pulled open the library door. He could hear Gilbert and Ned in the office, but he walked past them, directly to the master bedroom. The clothes he'd been wearing yesterday were in a pile on the floor on his side of the bed. Luckily Ned hadn't seen them yet, or they would have been spirited into a laundry bag somewhere. He sat on the bed and picked up the shorts, feeling the fabric. Sure enough, there was a wad of paper in the back pocket. He felt his heart pounding in his ears as he pulled it out. There were two torn-out newspaper clippings and a grease-stained pastry bag. One clipping was the article he had just read, and the other was an ad for the exhibition, with a picture of Gilbert's brooch. It had been more than a lucid dream.

Hands trembling, he unfolded the pastry bag and pulled it open. There were a few greasy crumbs in the bottom, and a smudge of chocolate. He put it up to his nose and inhaled: Boston cream. In a flood of images it all came back to him—the missing house, hitchhiking to the city, angry Hanh, vegan doughnuts, Danny and the surly bartender, and finally Laura rescuing him. A whole day in a different version of his city. A different time zone, Laura had called it.

He flopped back onto the bed and laughed loudly. He'd done it—slipped through time to figure out Gilbert's mystery, and even managed to remember. It was such a rush. The clippings and the pastry bag were tangible evidence—he still had no idea how he'd done it, but at least he remembered being there, and he had proof that it was real. It was a real-world experience, and it went way beyond the familiar realm of dreams and inspiration.

But he didn't really feel like he had any control over it. Laura had said he was complicit in the time shift, that he'd picked the parameters of the experience; but it hadn't been a conscious decision. And why would he have done that to himself? The disorientation had been terrifying. But in hindsight it had also been … not enjoyable, really, but certainly exciting.

He closed his eyes, lying on the bed and holding the greasy pastry bag, and for a moment had a feeling of vastness, like looking into the night sky, a sense of limitless possibility stretching out before him, waiting only for him to act. Maybe his psychic potential was just that—limitless.

Something nagged at the corner of his mind, something he was forgetting, or missing. In the diner Laura had explained as best she could what had happened, how Mason had wound up "out of sequence," as she put it, and even why Hanh was there too. But there was something else—what was it? He closed his eyes again and tried to clear his mind, to let information flow in.

The library. She had surreptitiously gone into Daniel's library at dinner. At the time he had assumed she was after the gold brooch, but it wasn't that. He opened his eyes and stuffed the newspaper clippings and the pastry bag into the back pocket of the pants he was wearing, then walked back to the library, closing the door behind him. There it was: *The Lost Weekend.* He pulled it out and fanned through the pages. It was still here, the little square of foil jammed in like a bookmark.

He pulled it out and looked it over, ran it

between his thumb and fingers, then folded it in half. This was definitely not what he'd found on Saturday. The first time he'd seen it, it felt like it was rubberized, and it had flattened itself out again when he creased it. This was regular old kitchen foil, for wrapping leftovers or grilling veggies. Laura must have swapped them when she snuck in here. But why? And why hadn't she mentioned it to him? He was going to have to talk to her—but he had no idea how to find her.

For now, though, he had to decide what to tell Gilbert—how to tell him that his father was almost certainly a thief, when Gilbert was still raw with grief. He'd found the same piece of information to answer Gilbert's question through two independent channels, and even though the information didn't provide a definitive answer—he hadn't seen Daniel actually stealing anything—it was more than enough to extrapolate the truth.

Mason spent some time reading through the news articles about the burglary and the investigation all those years ago, just to make sure he had a clear understanding of the sequence of events to take to Gilbert. Coverage had been frenzied when most of the stolen pieces were shipped back to the museum, and the whole incident was a boon for attendance—the exhibit had sold out for weeks. Despite the wild accusations and theories thrown around by the newspapers at the time, no one was ever arrested, and the investigation had gone cold.

A while later Ned pushed open the library

door. "I'm making some lunch, if you're hungry. Teriyaki tofu. How is your research going? Have you figured out what the pin thingy is?"

"I think I'm making progress," he hedged. "And lunch sounds great. I'll be right behind you."

Ned left the door ajar, and Mason waited long enough for him to get back to the kitchen. He walked quietly out into the hallway and looked into the office; Gilbert had abandoned the cramped space as well. As he'd hoped, Daniel's office printer also made photocopies. He pulled the newspaper clippings out of his pants and smoothed them out, making a copy of each and stuffing the originals back in his pocket.

"It's not that hot out today," Ned said from the kitchen when he walked in, "so we're going to eat outside." He handed Mason a big bowl of rice. "This goes on the patio table." Peggy was already outside, setting out plates and cutlery.

"Peggy, when do you have to be back at work?" Ned asked, following Gilbert out onto the patio and sliding the door closed behind them.

"Probably Tuesday," she said.

"Me too. I think maybe we can wrap things up tomorrow, and head out tomorrow night. Does that work?"

She and Mason both agreed, but Gilbert looked a little wistful.

"How's the writing?" Mason asked her.

"It's going well," she said, sitting down and pulling the chair close to the table. "I've finished one song and I'm working on another. Maybe I'll play something for you guys."

"I'd love that," Ned said.

"Maybe tonight after dinner," Peggy said. "My music likes dark corners and shadows. I don't think it would look so good in the harsh light of day."

MASON WAITED UNTIL AFTER they'd eaten to bring up the jewelry mystery.

"You know how we talked about the gold brooch, and how suspicious it was that it was hidden?" he began. He saw a flash of alarm in Gilbert's eyes. He'd been through a lot, and he probably knew it was going to be bad news.

"What have you found out?" Gilbert asked.

"The brooch was made 3,500 years ago in Turkey. It's Turkey now, but then it was the Hittite empire. They were Bronze Age people, kings and battles and all that. It was probably made for a king or queen, or maybe a lesser warlord, but definitely someone important, because it's a lot of gold. It was dug up in 1948 with a bunch of other jewelry from that era. It was a big deal then— they called it the hoard of something-or-other, the name of the place it was found. Eventually the collection of jewelry was loaned to museums all over the world, and in 1971 it came to Los Angeles."

"Mason, you did it," Peggy said, amazed. "You figured it out."

"There's more, though, isn't there?" Ned said quietly.

Mason passed the photocopies across the table to Gilbert, and Ned got up and stood behind his chair, reading over his shoulder.

"Oh, man," Gilbert said. "My dad did this. This says the pin was stolen from a museum truck when the collection was being moved. It had to be him." He looked at the second sheet, the ad for the exhibition with the photo of the brooch.

Mason was relieved that Gilbert had made the connection to Daniel, so he didn't have to spell it out for him.

"What is it?" Peggy asked Mason.

"Photocopies from an old newspaper," Mason said.

Ned said, "You can see it's definitely the same piece." Looking up at Mason, he asked, "Where did you get these?"

"I phoned in a favor at the library." It was only partly a lie. "That actually involves you, Gilbert. I got you a blind date."

"At least she'll know what kind of family I come from, if she found this," he said, passing the copies across to Peggy.

"The librarian just gave me access to the newspaper archives. I found the articles on my own, using psychic power. There are several more that I saved on my computer that I'll send to you."

"How did psychic power play into it?" Ned said, looking dubious.

"I had a kind of dream about it first, and that gave me the direction I needed to go hunting in the archives." He wasn't about to get into a debate, but he said, "Sparing you the technical complexities of it, I can assure you that it most definitely involved psychic power."

"Uh-huh," Ned said, unconvinced.

"Anyway," Mason said pointedly, "the other newspaper clippings from the time say that everything else that was stolen was returned anonymously to the museum before the exhibition even opened. And the investigation went cold—no one was ever arrested or charged."

"Maybe he had cohorts," Ned said. "Maybe someone in the group felt remorse and sent their share back."

"Or maybe Daniel did it alone, and sent everything back except one souvenir," Peggy said. She looked at Gilbert, who sat quietly, a thoughtful look on his face.

Finally he said, "I guess I'd buy that. He might have kept the pin as a reminder that he'd gotten away with it. He would have loved having a secret like that all to himself."

"There's still the possibility that it wasn't him," Mason said, "and that the brooch came to him some other way. But I can't find anything that suggests it was anyone else. One article said the movers worked for the museum, and they were questioned by the cops, of course, but the newspaper didn't name them. So nothing I've found says that he was there, but it doesn't exclude him being there either."

Gilbert said, "Ned, do you think in all that paperwork in his office there might be some record of him getting a paycheck from the museum, something like that?"

"I didn't see anything dating that far back. But you never know—I'll have a look today."

"Even if you don't find anything, it all seems to fit," Gilbert said. "I knew him well, and I hate to admit it, but it fits with who he was."

"So if it's safe to assume that he did steal it," Peggy said, "the next question is, what are you going to do with it?"

"I have no idea," Gilbert said, knitting his brow.

"Legally it belongs to whoever insured it, assuming they paid the claim," Ned said.

Mason said, "It was insured, but nobody ever saw a payout. A few years later the museum negotiated compensation with the Turks. So at least they got paid for it. Does that mean it belongs to the museum now?"

"I'm sure they would argue that it does," Ned said. "But I bet the Turks would want it back anyway."

"I suppose I can't just sell it," Gilbert said.

"You'd have no trouble finding a willing antiques dealer in the city," Ned said. "They'd see all that gold and snap it up, no questions asked, legal or not."

"If you sell it to some lowlife, and the gold is the focus, they might melt it down," Peggy said. "It's thousands of years old—that would be a tragic loss."

"More likely it would be resold to a private collector, don't you think?" Ned said. "It's worth more as an antique."

"But still, it would never be seen again," she said. "It might as well still be hidden in that flower-pot."

"I think you're all kind of missing the point," Mason said. "We've basically discovered a crime. You have to take it to the cops, and let them sort it out."

"But the person who committed the crime is dead," Ned said. "What possible benefit could there be in going to the police?"

"It's the right thing to do," Mason said simply.

"And it might get back into a museum that way," Peggy said.

"Or it might get caught up in international lawsuits for decades," Ned said. "That almost seems like sealing it up in a plant pot for another fifty years."

"But that's not our call," Mason said. "It might go back to Turkey eventually, or stay here, but either way it would be on display, so anyone could go see it. That seems like the best outcome, doesn't it?"

Gilbert said, "It just seems like it's so valuable, and I'm the one who found it. Why shouldn't I benefit from it?"

"Because it's not yours," Mason said sharply.

"Mason, you're being extremely conscientious," Ned said. "But to me that would be throwing away an opportunity, or giving the opportunity to someone else."

"Think about the bigger picture," Mason said calmly. "If you sell it, it's the same as sealing it up in plaster of paris, the way Daniel did. He obviously didn't need to sell it, or he would have. You said his estate has enough money for you to be comfortable for a while, so Gilbert, you don't really need to sell it either. If you give it back, it becomes something for everyone to admire and enjoy."

Peggy smiled faintly and met his eye, but Ned just looked annoyed.

Gilbert sighed. "I'll think about it." He looked tired.

Ned looked at Mason and said, "Are you going to let him make the decision, or are you going to make it for him?"

"Are you asking if I'll go to the cops regardless of what Gilbert wants to do?"

Ned raised his eyebrows in assent.

"It would be completely immoral to undermine a friend like that." Mason shot Ned a look, then turned to Gilbert. "Whatever you decide to do, you don't have to worry about me. I'll keep my mouth shut."

"OK," Gilbert said, but he didn't sound convinced.

Mason felt his face redden. "I have to be able to live with myself, man, and that means not screwing people over."

"All right," Peggy said. "Enough. Mason, we have a date to meet my brother. Gilbert, can I borrow your dad's pickup?"

"Can you drive a stick?"

"Sure."

"Then go ahead. It may look like it's on its last legs, but that thing is tough. You can go sixty on the bumpy part of the road in, and you won't even feel it."

HALF AN HOUR LATER Peggy and Mason climbed into Daniel's pickup. It started up for her instantly, the engine loud but sounding healthy.

"Look at this," she said, flopping the heavy gearshift back and forth. "All the numbers are worn off." It took her a minute of gently experimenting with the clutch to figure out where the gears were, and after she'd found low gear, she pulled out onto the road. "One up, two down, reverse down on the right," she said. "Help me remember that."

"You sound like one of those old vinyl records that taught people how to foxtrot. How many gears can there possibly be?"

"Cut me some slack, Mason. My car has a sewing-machine motor and push buttons, so this big old thing is intimidating," she said, clearly irritated.

"I'm not giving you a hard time," he said, laughing.

"Sorry. I'm feeling a bit stressed out lately. Writing a song about the breakup with Van keeps me in that head space for hours at a time."

"Are you nervous about meeting your brother too?"

"Yeah, I guess I am. I can't help wondering what it's going to be like. What if he's a crazy person?"

"You've already talked to him, and there was no indication of that, right? You said he sounded pretty ordinary."

"True," she admitted. "But think about what's at stake. He's my only connection to my dad. Meeting him could change everything that I know about myself."

"I don't think that's likely. You've already established yourself as sane and stable, regardless of what your blood relations are like."

"Let's hope so," she said, frowning out at the landscape ahead.

She reached the end of Daniel's road and swung the truck onto the highway, shifting up and accelerating. It looked the same as it had yesterday when he'd been hitchhiking, Mason thought. Or was it yesterday? In Laura's words, he had definitely been "out of sequence." He looked over at Peggy and considered telling her about it. She was gripping the steering wheel intently, her knuckles white. She had enough on her mind today, he decided. But he knew she was probably the only one who might believe him.

He looked out at the passing desert and realized he was ready for a nap. It felt like jet lag—he'd been up and awake so early, and now he was ready for bed. Maybe Laura's analogy about traversing time zones was more apt than he'd thought.

The desert scrub was flashing by awfully quickly. "Jesus, Peggy, are we late?" He glanced over at the speedometer, but it was bobbing at zero. "You must be going eighty," he said, raising his voice to be heard over the road noise.

She looked at him, perplexed. "Why would I slow down? There's no traffic here at all."

"Oh," Mason said. She wasn't speeding because of her nerves; it was just because she could. Sometimes he thought he was the only Angeleno who didn't love driving. He leaned toward her and said, "I wish they all could be California girls."

She found the coffeehouse along the town's lone commercial strip, a short stretch of the main highway. She parked on a side street and switched off the engine. Mason got out, and Peggy opened her door, but she just sat in the driver's seat, staring into space.

"Are you OK?" Mason asked, after walking around to her side.

"So we're really doing this," she said.

"It'll be fine, sweetie. You know how you can get up in front of a bar full of people and play guitar for them? It's like that, only a lot easier because it's just one guy, and presumably he'll be sober."

"Yeah, I guess so." She nodded, and after a moment climbed out, and they set off toward the front door.

The interior of the coffeehouse was done up in rustic Old West style, with timeworn mining tools, oil lanterns, and wagon wheels mounted on the weathered wooden walls. Mason wondered if it was intentional, or if everything just looked that way out here.

He spotted Peggy's brother before she did, sitting at a table over by the wall. Peggy saw him too, and he heard her inhale sharply.

"Here we go," she said, and walked over to him.

Mason saw recognition in his face when he looked up at her. He had the same eyes, the same brown hair—there was no mistaking that they were related.

"Peggy?" he said, rising from his chair.

"Andy. You look so familiar, even though we've never met. How crazy is that?" She smiled and held out her hand.

"I think we're beyond the handshake stage," he said, and gave her a quick hug.

Mason introduced himself and shook his hand.

"Call me Andy," he said. "I only go by Andrew for work."

Peggy sat across from him, and Mason took a chair at the end of the table, watching as they took each other in. Andy laughed nervously, and Peggy fidgeted, her cheeks bright pink.

"It's so freaky," Andy said. "You look like my dad. Seeing you in the flesh, there's not a shred of doubt left in my mind." Shifting focus to Mason, he said, "So you're the man who brought us together. It certainly blindsided me. How did you do it?"

"Well, I work as an investigator," Mason began.

"I told him about your research at the library," Peggy cut in, emphasizing *library.* Mason took her cue to leave out the part about psychic power. She probably didn't want to make the long-lost-sister story even more bizarre.

Andy said, "Well, I'm glad you figured it out. More people means a richer life, right?"

"It sounds like you're an optimist," Peggy said.

They really were a lot alike, Mason saw, watching them chat as their initial nervousness faded. Before long he felt his eyelids drooping, and said, "I'm going to get coffee."

"Can you get me a soy latte?" Peggy asked.

He went up to the counter and nodded to the barista, a young guy with a short beard, his hair tied up in a topknot. "What can I get you?" he said, with a perfunctory smile.

"A quadruple espresso, and a soy latte."

He raised his eyebrows and looked at Mason. "You're not from around here, are you?"

"Is it that obvious?"

"Well, we don't have soy milk. And I've never

heard anyone order a quadruple anything."

"OK, then, I'll have two double espressos, poured into the same cup. Or four single espressos, if that's easier. And you can make the latte with regular old coyote milk."

The barista laughed. "Take it easy, man. I know what 'quadruple' means. I can make your latte with almond milk, will that work?"

"Yes," Mason said, chastened. He hadn't meant to snap at the guy, but he'd been awake for too long.

"The owner keeps it around for a guy who's lactose intolerant." He set about making the espresso, chuckling to himself.

"What's so funny?" Mason asked.

"Coyote milk," the barista said, from behind the espresso machine. "I'm guessing you're from LA?"

"How could you possibly know that? Is it the shoes?" Mason asked, looking down at his orange sneakers.

"No, it's the attitude—that's an urban thing, that kind of sarcasm. Coyote milk." He chuckled again. Even though he had called Mason out, he didn't seem offended. "In a town this size, everyone knows everyone, so you have to work harder here to maintain good relationships. If you start alienating people, pretty soon you won't have anyone."

Mason considered that for a moment. "I actually know a lot of people who do that, cycling through friends, ditching them when they don't live up to their expectations. In a city of ten million people, there's an unlimited supply of new ones."

"So you live stacked on top of each other like firewood, but you don't really need social skills. In a small town you need to be much more sophisticated to get along. Socially, anyway." He set two cups down in front of Mason. "Nine fifty."

"You certainly don't charge unsophisticated prices," Mason said, pulling a wad of bills out of his pocket and peeling off a ten. "Seriously, though, I appreciate your perspective. It's insightful."

"I just think it's important to point out to city people that small communities may be provincial, but that doesn't mean simple. And hey, you gave me a name for the bar that I'm going to open. Coyote Milk. Can I use it?"

"It's yours," Mason said, and smiled to himself as he walked back to Peggy and Andy.

The two of them were deep in an animated conversation about the music industry. They even had the same body language, he realized, waving their hands around and leaning forward for emphasis. Mason handed Peggy her latte and sat and sipped his espresso, listening politely.

The conversation turned more serious when Peggy asked about their father. Andy talked about his character, this man who had never even known of Peggy's existence, her father by blood alone. Her eyes brimmed with tears, but she held it together, listening intently and asking questions.

"Sorry, Mason, we've been ignoring you," Andy said finally.

"Today's about you two. I'm just happy you were up here this weekend."

"It is an odd coincidence, that we both wind up in the nonexistent Natron, California, on the same weekend," Andy said. "Maybe it's kismet."

Peggy must have become comfortable enough with Andy, because she said, "Mason thinks the two of us arranged it subconsciously."

"That's sounds very New Age," Andy said.

"That term implies spiritual beliefs," Mason said, eyeing him carefully. "But it's not that."

Peggy said, "It's Mason's business to know about these things—he works as a psychic investigator. It's how he found you for me."

"Seriously?" Andy said, looking from her to Mason.

"Yeah, it's serious," Mason said. "I haven't been doing it for that long, but I seem to be getting better at it."

"So what exactly do you investigate?" Andy asked. He seemed interested, Mason was happy to note, rather than dismissive as so many people were.

"So far, I've found people. And I figured out the provenance of a piece of ancient jewelry, just this weekend." Mason dug around in his pants pocket and pulled out his business card, passing it to Andy.

"'Psychic investigator.' How cool is that?" Andy said, examining it. "So how did you psychically find the link between Peggy and me?"

"I was digging around in the library, like Peggy said, and one night I had this flash. Kind of an inspiration. It was about the nightclub where your father and her mother worked back in the day. I went to the library and found his picture in an old newspaper. The family resemblance was unmistakable."

"I wouldn't have believed it if I wasn't sitting here living it," Andy said. "There are more things going on in the world than we'll ever know."

"Exactly," Peggy said.

"You should come over to my cabin. There's something going on there that I just don't understand—a *woo-woo* kind of thing. It might be interesting for you to check it out."

"What kind of thing?" Peggy asked. "Not the local Sasquatch—please tell me you haven't seen that."

"Nothing like that," Andy said, and smiled. "Rather than explain it, I think it's probably better for you just to experience it directly. I can't guarantee that it'll happen, of course, but it happens almost every night I'm there."

Peggy looked at Mason. "What do you think?"

"I'm intrigued," he said. "But is it anything dangerous? There's no chance of losing a finger or anything?"

Andy laughed. "It doesn't involve power tools,

and it's not all that frightening. That's if it happens at all—and if it doesn't, it's a good excuse to hang out at my place and drink beer. You can meet my dog, Rufus."

"I'm in," said Mason.

"Yeah," Peggy said. "Let's do it."

"Do you have a map program on your phone?" Andy asked.

"Mason does."

"Let me mark my place for you. It doesn't really have a street address."

Mason passed his phone over, and Andy fiddled with it for a moment. "It's right there," he said, "a few miles down a side road off the main highway."

Mason took the phone back and looked at the map. "That's really close to Daniel's place," he said, zooming out. "It can't be more than three miles, as the crow flies. It looks like it's just across the valley, on the other side of the arroyo."

Peggy took the phone and looked at the map. "I bet it's the place you can see off in the distance from Daniel's patio."

"Have you ever met Laura, the woman who camps on the arroyo, near the hand pump?" Mason asked.

"Yeah, she dropped by my cabin last winter."

"She used to drop in on Daniel too," Mason said. "I don't suppose you'd know how to get in touch with her?"

Peggy shot him a questioning look.

Andy said, "No idea. She's a bit odd, but nice enough."

"We just had dinner with her," Peggy said, "and I think she's very odd. She seems to have moved on—her trailer wasn't there this morning."

Mason took his phone back, and looked at the map again. If his reckoning was accurate, the well on the arroyo where Laura camped was almost exactly halfway between Daniel's place and Andy's cabin. That had to be more than a coincidence.

Peggy finished her coffee, and they made plans to meet at Andy's cabin later that evening.

"Bring your jackets," he said. "It's starting to cool off at night."

They said their good-byes and headed out to the street. When they climbed back into the pickup, Peggy put both hands on the steering wheel and exhaled deeply.

"So how was that?" Mason asked.

"I feel relieved," she said. "And energized too. You were right—he's an ordinary guy."

"And he's not a skeptic, so I personally love him already."

She started the truck and aimed it back onto the highway, fumbling a little at first to find the right gears. "I wonder what the hell is going on at his cabin that he wants us to see. That's the only thing that seems a bit strange. Although I think he knows that, because he used the technical term *woo-woo*."

"I love that too—he's got a mystery to share with you."

"But he couldn't even describe it."

"That's actually a kindness to us. It means he's got a truly open mind. If he had put a label on it for us, we couldn't be objective about it. This way, we won't have any preconceived ideas when we go over there."

"Well, whatever it is, you're probably the guy to figure it out."

"How'd it go?" Ned greeted them when they walked into the house. He was in the front room, feet up on the coffee table, one of Daniel's old hardbound books splayed open on the sofa beside him.

Peggy said, "Pretty great. He's a sweet guy."

"And he looks a lot like her," Mason added. "It's almost eerie."

"I wouldn't have used that word," Peggy said, "but there is a strong resemblance."

"We're going over to his cabin later tonight to drink beer," Mason said.

Peggy looked at Mason, a question in her eyes, but she didn't elaborate about Andy's real reason for inviting them over. "Where's Gilbert?" she asked.

"Having a nap. I think the sheer volume of stuff to do is overwhelming his brain. But I'll wake him up for dinner. I'm thinking a really thin pizza crust, so thin you could read a book through it, with some artichokes and black olives."

"Hell, yes," Peggy said. "Speaking of beer, do we have any?"

"In the door of the fridge," Ned said. "Bring it in here and tell me all about your brother."

Mason left them to talk and went into the master bedroom to lie down. Gilbert had the right idea; he was exhausted, and Ned would surely wake him for dinner.

He thought about the events of the day, and then about the little bit of foil in *The Lost Week-end,* and whether it had any connection to Laura. Maybe he could intuit it, he thought, the way she had relentlessly encouraged him to. He closed his eyes and realized he was very close to sleep. He'd never tried it before, but maybe he could go even farther and communicate with her directly with his mind. Of all people, Laura should be able to pick up that kind of message; she seemed to be unhindered by the rules of reality that most people agreed on—even the flow of time. He cleared his mind and focused on the emptiness. *Why would you take a little piece of foil?* he thought, casting the words out into the void. *I have so many questions for you. Come back and talk to me.*

He must have drifted off, because he woke up to Ned gently rubbing his arm. It was dark out.

"Are you hungry?" Ned asked.

"What time is it?" He felt groggy.

"Almost seven. There's food."

"I'm in," Mason said, sitting up, trying to wake up completely.

He followed Ned to the kitchen, where Peggy was setting out forks and glasses. Ned had made four lovely dinner plate–size pizzas.

Gilbert was already at the table. "My god, man, how do you do this? It looks like it's been cooked in a wood oven."

"It's all about high heat," Ned said, and sat down with them.

"So, Mason," Gilbert said, "don't think I forgot about my blind date. What is this woman like?"

"She's a librarian, like I said, and her name is Harmony. Curvy, buxom …"

Gilbert nodded. "Just my type."

"A little bit materialistic, I think. She's got a Jamaican vibe going on. Caribbean accent, and wears her hair in dreadlocks."

"I'm already fascinated," Gilbert said. From the expression on his face, Mason could tell he was being sincere.

After they'd eaten, Ned pushed his plate away. Looking serious, he said, "So I dug into Daniel's records. His business was set up several years after the jewelry heist."

"That means he wasn't working for himself yet," Gilbert said. "He would have been working on someone else's crew."

"It's still not really evidence that he did it," Ned said, "but it doesn't contradict it either."

"I don't have any doubt anymore that he stole that damn thing. I think I just needed some time to absorb the idea," Gilbert said, folding his arms. "Anyway, what did you think of Peggy's bro, Mason? Is he as hot as her?"

"He seems like a nice guy, but I wouldn't call him hot. He's straight, right, and straight guys aren't really hot."

"Oh, you wish," Gilbert said, a lurid grin on his face.

Peggy told Gilbert a little about her brother, and then said, "Listen—a couple of the songs I've written are ready for public consumption. I want to play them for you guys."

"That's exciting," Ned said.

"Can we go into the front room? Let me grab my guitar."

Mason picked up his chair and followed Ned and Gilbert into the front room. She usually performed while perched on a stool, he knew, and the comfy chairs in there wouldn't allow her to work her guitar and project her voice.

Peggy sat on the kitchen chair, and they waited quietly while she adjusted her guitar. Something seemed off about her as she set up; it took Mason a moment to realize it was that she wasn't wearing her huge fake pregnant belly. Finally she strummed a few chords, and seemed satisfied with the sound.

"I wrote this first one before I broke up with Van. It's called 'Wildflowers,'" she said, and started into the song's bright, cheerful lead-in. Mason loved hearing her play at such close proximity— he could enjoy the emotion of the music rather than being distracted by the crowd in a club. She launched into the first verse:

> You and me, little one
> Bendin' in the wind like wildflowers
> Stay with me today
> Our moments becoming hours.

It was classic Peggy Pregnant—sweet, romantic lyrics and an upbeat folk melody. She sang a few more verses, and ended the last chord with a flourish, then smiled at them.

Gilbert clapped loudly, leaning forward in his easy chair, a broad, idiotic grin on his face.

"It's beautiful," Mason said.

"Yeah," Ned said. "It has so much impact."

"Thanks, guys. It's not too light?"

"Not at all—it's lovely," Ned said.

"I guess it just seems vacuous because I've been in a darker place since I wrote it."

"I wouldn't change a thing," Mason said. "I can easily imagine you playing that on stage. People will love it."

"Good to hear." She nodded and twanged a string. "So the other one I've been working on is newer. It's called 'Skid Mark.' It's a breakup song, so it's a little dark."

Ned said, "I think we can handle it," and smiled encouragingly.

"OK, but I want more feedback after."

It had a long lead-in, and the melody was sad, but it didn't drag.

> Of course your mama named you Van
> More of a skid mark than a man
> You left tread marks on my heart
> When you peeled out on the asphalt of our love.

Mason looked over at Ned. He looked surprised, and met Mason's eyes for a moment. This was nothing like Peggy's sweet folk style. Was she being serious?

She strummed through another nonverbal section, and then her voice rose again.

> Wheels keep going 'round
> But the very thought of you just brings me down
> Everything tastes like rancid lunch meat
> Since you peeled out on the asphalt of our love.

Mason watched her closely as she played. She was definitely not joking. The song had a few more verses, and another stretch of guitar work. Finally it was over, and Gilbert clapped again, but Mason and Ned just sat in stunned silence.

"The imagery," Ned managed finally. "It's so ... vivid."

"Thank you," she said. "I wondered if it was too dark, but you think it works?"

"Uh ..."

"You said his name in the song. Can you do that?" Mason asked. "Isn't that libel?"

"What's he going to do, sue me? I say, bring it on, motherfucker."

"Such passion," Gilbert said, delight in his voice.

"I liked the first one better," Mason said.

Peggy said, "Most important is the melody. Do you think that works?"

"That part is great," Ned said.

Gilbert asked, "What made you think of lunch meat?"

"I guess it just seemed like something gross, and that was how I was feeling."

"I'd love to hear the other songs you're planning to put on your EP," Ned said. "It would give us a better overall sense of it."

"Sure," she said. "Mason, what did you think?"

"Well … the melody works, as Ned said. The lyrics are so … I guess, visceral?"

"Good. I'm glad that comes through."

"It does. And, hey, I also think we should hit the road soon—Andy will be expecting us." He didn't know what else to say about the song. Maybe he'd think of a way to critique it diplomatically later on.

"Yes, it's probably that time. Thanks for listening, guys, and thanks for the feedback. Do you two want to come along and meet my brother?"

"Not tonight," Gilbert said.

Ned said, "I'm sure I'll meet Andy eventually, but I'm staying here too."

As Peggy left to put her guitar away and get

ready, Mason remembered Andy's suggestion to bring a jacket. "Gilbert, does your dad have a coat that I can borrow?"

"Sure." He led Mason to a closet near the front door. "Take your pick."

Mason dug through several and found a baggy, flannel-lined work jacket. "I'm thinking this one," he said, pulling it on.

"You can keep it, if it fits."

"Thanks, man. But I feel weird taking it."

"Don't. My dad's not going to miss it." He straightened the collar, nodding approvingly, so close that Mason could smell his hair. It was too intimate, and for a second he thought that Gilbert might try to kiss him. That would be such a Gilbert thing to do. But instead he stepped back and looked Mason in the eye. "Do psychics ever talk to dead people?"

"I know lots of them claim to," he said. "It might be possible to connect with some part of a dead person's essence, or some other version of them. But I think when people die, they're just gone."

"Good to know." He nodded but looked away. "I think I know that, in my gut, but it's reassuring to hear it from someone who's psychic."

Mason nodded. "Do you have unfinished business with your dad?"

"Well, I'd love to ask him how he stole that damn pin, and why he baked it into a flower pot, but other than that, no. I think I said everything to him that I needed to say."

"You're lucky, then," Mason said, and squeezed Gilbert's arm.

"I guess I am."

PEGGY FIRED UP THE pickup and they roared off up the road, Mason navigating with his phone. Soon they were at the dirt road that led to Andy's place—a much more primitive road than Daniel's, and the house was a lot farther off the highway. Peggy drove slowly in the dark, leaning over the steering wheel for a better view in the wan light cast by the old pickup's headlights. Mason thought of the night they had arrived, passing their doppelgängers on the way to Daniel's. He was definitely going to revisit that with Peggy. Finally they came to the end of the road and Andy's cabin. The yard light was on, and as they pulled up Andy stepped out the door and waved. Close behind him was a red-coated dog, barking and wagging its tail.

"This is Rufus," Andy explained as they climbed out of the truck, and the animal ran over and excitedly stiffed at them both.

His cabin really was a cabin, not a sprawling country house like Daniel's place. It was definitely home to a single man, Mason noticed, with beat-up furniture and haphazard piles of clothes, paper, and boxes.

"Excuse the mess," Andy said, leading them to the side of the room with a fridge and a rudimentary kitchen sink. "I haven't been up here in months."

"It's not really a mess," Peggy said. "Just well lived in."

Andy laughed, and pulled two bottles of beer from the fridge, handing them to his guests, then pulling out another.

"Ooh, fancy," Peggy said, admiring the label.

"It's not expensive, but it is imported," he said. He popped the caps off and said, "I hope you don't mind drinking out of the bottle—I don't know if I could even find two clean glasses."

Peggy said, "Of course not," and they followed him out the back door of the cabin, where there was a wrought-iron table between a couple of Adirondack chairs, and a sun lounger off to one side.

Mason headed for the lounger, glad he had worn a jacket, as it was cooler outside than it had been. He sat down and twisted his bottle gently into the gravel.

Andy switched off the lights before he sat down, and Rufus stretched out at his feet. "We'll be able to see better once we've been out here for a little while," he said. Mason could already see a lot of stars.

"So I take it your mystery happens out here," Peggy said.

Andy said, "It might take a while. I have a feeling it'll happen, though."

Mason sipped his beer and scanned the darkness. He couldn't see the landscape yet, but there was a fuzzy, dim light in the distance. "That must be Daniel's house," he said.

"It's so weird that you're staying right over there, within sight of my place, just when we decided we should get together," Andy said. "Mason, you thought maybe we arranged it sub-consciously. How does that work?"

"I'm not exactly sure," Mason said. "But I think your mind works on more levels than you're aware of, planning things and acting things out, or calling your conscious attention to places or events. So maybe a deeper part of your mind brought you both out here."

Mason looked over at them, but in the darkness could only see vague silhouettes. Andy didn't reply, and they sat in comfortable silence.

Eventually Peggy asked Andy about his music, and Mason only half listened as they got into it. He was comfortable, and warm; he let his mind drift away from their conversation. He wished he had a better answer for Andy. But he didn't really know how he was doing what he was doing, despite his success with it. Maybe it was like a toddler learn-ing to walk; trial and error, just doing it, seemed to be the path he was on. Sometimes he wished he had an instructor, or at least a lesson plan.

In the darkness, dimmer stars gradually filled in the spaces among the bright ones. Part of the Milky Way was visible, intricate clumps of brighter and darker sky. It was relaxing just watching those myriad points of light, almost like meditating.

Peggy stopped talking in mid-sentence. Somewhere over the arroyo a blue light had appeared, drifting lazily upward. It was a dull, intense cobalt blue, not blue-white like a streetlight, and not bright like the stars. Mason felt his skin prickle.

"Are you seeing this?" Peggy asked quietly.

"Oh, yeah," Mason said. "It's the light Gilbert was talking about."

"What is it?" Peggy asked, her voice tense.

"That's the mystery," Andy said. "I was hoping the psychic investigator might have some insight."

The dog growled, softly and low in his throat, clearly aware that something was awry.

"Rufus, quiet," Andy said.

Mason was certain it had something to do with Laura and her obtuse activities. The light drifted upward, not randomly like a balloon, but on an arcing, purposeful path. Maybe it would be possible to read the light remotely, he thought, rather than the hands-on way he did with jewelry. Mason stared at it and cleared his mind, trying to make room for insight about it while he focused on it. It stopped in its path, as if it were aware, as if it had sensed his interest. His heart started pounding faster, but he maintained his focus on the light. Was it getting bigger now?

"Are you seeing this? It's coming over here," Peggy said.

Mason tried to open his mind to get insight, the way Laura had encouraged him to, while focusing his attention on the light. If it was under intelligent control, maybe he could learn what that intelligence wanted to say. But despite its change in course, he wasn't picking up anything.

It was hard to gauge how close the thing had come, but it was bigger than a point of light now, clearly circular.

"It's not going to do anything to us, is it?" Peggy asked.

"It never has," Andy said. "Sometimes there are more than one—" As he spoke the words, a second blue light appeared, lower over the arroyo.

"Another one," Peggy said. "Mason, what are you getting?"

"Nada," he said, staring at the lights, no longer trying to focus his mind on them. "Would you say they're spherical? I can't see that, but I kind of feel it."

"Yeah, I get that too," Andy said.

They watched in silence while the orbs drifted and looped around the sky. Mason tried again to quiet his mind and get some inspiration about them, but there was just nothing. Eventually one of them winked out, then the other.

"Are they coming back?" Peggy asked.

Andy said, "It's hard to say. They might be gone for the evening."

"They're not gone. Look," Mason said. Out on the arroyo, below the level of Daniel's light, were a pair of yellow-white lights.

"Oh, yeah," Andy said. "They look like headlights, don't they? Maybe it's your friend Laura camping out there again."

"They're too far apart to be headlights," Peggy said.

None of them said anything, and they watched the lights, which didn't move or even waver, for what seemed like ages. Finally they winked off, one slightly before the other. They were quiet for a few minutes, but nothing else came to interrupt the vast dome of stars overhead.

"That might be it," Andy said tentatively.

"You certainly know how to throw a party," Peggy said.

"I told you it was a mystery," he said. "Mason, any insights?"

"I do have a theory, but you won't believe it."

"Try me," Andy said.

"Yeah, tell us," Peggy said.

He took a long pull from his beer bottle. "OK. On Saturday night I had an unusual experience. You could call it a dream, I guess, but it was an extremely vivid dream."

"A psychic vision?"

"That sounds right." He thought for a moment about how to phrase it. "So in this vision, I met Laura, and she was a lot more rational than she had been at dinner. She told me that she was working out there, and now I think the lights we just saw are a side effect of that."

"Working? Doing what?" Peggy asked.

"I didn't exactly understand it, but she said

she was trying to fix some problem with the structure of reality. She compared herself to a cable TV repair person, only she was repairing space-time."

"You're right," Andy said. "That's a stretch."

"But it was a vision," Peggy said, "so it wasn't real. She didn't actually tell you that."

"I think she actually did. It was dreamlike, but I think she was really there," Mason said. "I knew you wouldn't believe it."

"I'm not saying I don't believe it," Peggy said. "Just give me a minute."

Mason looked over at their vague outlines in the darkness, both sitting in silence. He could almost hear Peggy's mind working.

Finally Peggy said, "So the lights are connected to her work, repair work, like sparks coming off a welding torch, something like that?"

"Right. I'm certain the lights are connected to her."

"I wonder if she's an alien?" Peggy said. "Wouldn't that be the ultimate cosmic joke, that Gilbert is obsessed with aliens, and with women, and then he unwittingly falls for an alien woman?"

"I asked her that, and she says she's not. She claims she's just a person who can move through time differently than the rest of us, and be in more than one place at the same time."

"Well, at dinner she did seem like a space cadet," Peggy said. "I guess it sort of makes sense as a reason for that. But it all happened in a dream, Mason. Are you sure about this?"

"I know it sounds crazy, but that's what I re-member."

"Andy, you're being awfully quiet," Peggy said. "Have we blown your mind?"

"I guess it's a lot to take in. But I've seen those blue lights many times over the years, and Mason's explanation is no less believable than anything I've come up with on my own."

"Fair enough," she said. "It sounds like you're keeping an open mind."

"Always," he said. "Listen, I'm going to grab another one of these. Are either of you ready for another?"

"Sure," Mason said, "but can you do it with-out turning on the lights? I'm enjoying the star-light."

"When it comes to beer, I could find it blind-folded," he said.

They had another round, and talked about other things. Mason felt better, lighter, having talked about his experiences. He hadn't told them everything, and he'd distorted the fact that it had been very real, rather than a vision or a dream, but still, it was liberating to talk about it.

Eventually Peggy said, "It's getting late. Thanks for the beer, bro."

"I'm glad you could come over," Andy said, walking back to the house and turning on the lights, which seemed blinding now. "And Mason, thanks for shedding some light on the mystery orbs."

"I don't know if I've done that," he said, rising from the lounger and shielding his eyes from the light.

"It's the best explanation I've heard yet," Andy said, and grinned. He walked them to the front of the house, then crouched there as they left, holding Rufus's collar so the dog wouldn't chase after the truck.

PEGGY DROVE SLOWLY AWAY from Andy's, picking up speed once they were back on the highway.

"Did you tell Ned about the whole psychic vision thing with Laura?" she asked.

"Nope. Do you think I should?"

"That's not for me to say. I wonder how he'd react."

"I know exactly how he'd react," Mason said. "Disbelief. But what can I say? I hardly believe it myself."

When Mason went into the master bedroom, Ned was shirtless and under the sheets, propped up on the pillows with one of Daniel's old hardcover books in hand, another old movie playing softly on the TV.

"How did it go?" he asked, setting the book down in his lap.

"It was fun," Mason said, kicking off his sneakers and climbing onto the bed.

"He's a good guy?"

"I think so, yeah. I liked him. He's quite open-minded."

"So you told him about your psychic thing," Ned said, shifting position and putting his arm around Mason's back.

"I did. He asked how I'd found him. He's not skeptical at all."

"Well, you did find him, there's no disputing that."

"Hey, do you remember Gilbert talking about seeing weird blue lights over the arroyo? We saw them tonight. We were sitting outside in the dark, and they appeared and floated around in the sky."

"Seriously? What do you think they were?"

"No clue. But a theory was proposed that it had something to do with Laura."

"I'm assuming you're the one who developed that theory," Ned said.

Mason looked at him for a moment. "You know me pretty well."

"Who else would have come up with that?"

"Well, Peggy called her a space cadet. Andy met her, and he said she was odd too."

"But only Mason could come up with a theory like that," he said, and climbed up, straddling him. "My crazy raspberry man."

"You don't mind the crazy so much when it's sexy time," Mason said, grabbing his hands and pulling him down for a kiss.

AFTER THEY'D HAD SEX and he was drifting into sleep, Mason dreamed again that he was floating in darkness. A bright star shone just outside his vision, illuminating the landscape far below him. It wasn't a star, he realized, trying to turn toward it and squinting at it, but a flickering projector bulb, with transparent, image-laden film drifting in front of it, stretching off in all directions. It was vivid enough that he made himself wake up and scrabble around for his pen and notepad. "floating—projector—film—landscape," he scrawled, and fell back asleep.

Monday

SOMETIME MID-MORNING, PEGGY STUCK her head into the bedroom and woke Mason.

"If you want to eat, you should come now," she said. "You smell that? Freshly baked bread, baby."

"Damn," he groaned. The heady aroma filled the air, too much to resist. He rolled out of bed and got dressed, joined the others at the kitchen table, and admired the spread.

"I'm kind of bummed you guys have to leave today," Gilbert said, spooning jam onto his toast.

Ned said, "You'll be back in town soon enough. It'll be good to get out of here, back to your regular life. You'll bury your dad, and then move on."

"Jesus, Ned—isn't that a little insensitive?" Peggy said.

"He's right, though," Gilbert said. "The funeral is the next step."

"I'm just trying to be frank," Ned said. "It doesn't mean I'm minimizing his grief."

"OK," she said, and cut herself another chunk of bread. "Gilbert, did you notice your girlfriend is camping out on the arroyo again? She wasn't gone for long. I guess she can't stay away from you."

"Don't encourage him," Ned said.

"Really, she's back?" Mason said, getting up quickly and looking around the room. "Where did we leave the binoculars?"

"They're on the table outside," Peggy said.

"Why do you care?" Ned said, frowning.

Mason ignored him and slid open the glass door, holding the binoculars to his eyes. He broke into a grin. It was her, all right, the blue car and shiny perfect Airstream. She must have heard him.

Gilbert came out and stood beside him, glowering suspiciously. "Let me see."

Mason handed over the glasses, and Gilbert held them to his eyes.

"You're right, her rig is back," Gilbert said, "and right in the same place.... Holy balls, she's walking over here." He set the binoculars down with a clatter and hurried toward the back of the house.

"What about your breakfast?" Ned called after him.

"No time," he called back. He returned a minute later wearing black chinos and a collared shirt, his hair slicked back.

"Much better," Ned said. "Now you look like a bank teller."

The doorbell rang, and Gilbert darted to the front door. A moment later he was back in the kitchen, a goofy smile on his face, with Laura, who was still dressed for camping. Ned stood to greet her.

"Don't get up, you're eating," she said. "How is everyone?"

"We're just finishing up," Ned said. "Can I get you a coffee, or some bread?"

"No, thanks."

"Don't you look pretty in plaid," Peggy said. "It brings out your eyes."

"Thank you, sweetie," she said, and smiled.

Ned looked at Peggy and mouthed, "Meow."

Mason looked her over carefully. She seemed present and engaged, much as she had in the city, not distracted and spacey as she had been at dinner.

"I'm actually here to see Mason. If you have a minute, Mason, I'd like to speak to you privately."

"I was hoping you'd drop by," Mason said.

"About what?" Gilbert said, scowling now.

"I have some ongoing business with Mason, but it won't take too long. Maybe you and I can hang out later today or tomorrow, Gilbert, how does that sound?"

"Great," he said, surprised.

"Maybe we can talk in Daniel's library?" she said to Mason. "Although I guess it's Gilbert's library now."

"Sure," Mason said, and grabbed the half-eaten piece of bread from his plate to take with him.

Ned caught his eye, raising his eyebrows to ask, *What's going on?*

Mason shrugged as he left, feigning ignorance. He felt a twinge of guilt about keeping so much from Ned. He knew he'd have to explain himself eventually, but how?

Mason followed Laura into the library and closed the door behind them. He waited for her to sit down in one of the wing chairs before taking the other, facing her.

"I thought you might drop by if I asked you to," he said. "And you seem to be all here. You're not also in 1940 or something, are you?"

"I'm here," she said, and grinned. "It seems like you've remembered everything about your little excursion the other day."

"It took a while, but yeah, it all came back. It seemed very real."

"It was real. You actually bled through to that time, your mind and body and everything. It's a remarkable achievement."

"Thanks, I guess … but I don't feel like I have any control over it. It happened without any planning or anything."

"You'll get better at it. I can't say you'll ever be able to consciously control it, but I suspect you'll develop it into a skill that you can use in your work."

Mason got up and walked over to the bookshelf and *The Lost Weekend*. He pulled the book out and sat down again, riffling through the pages to find the piece of foil. Watching her carefully, he passed it across to her.

She took it, and met his gaze, but didn't react.

"So I have to ask you," he said, "why you swiped that other little piece of aluminum."

She waved the foil in the air and laughed. "So you figured that out. I assume I have you to thank for finding it in the first place."

"I did find it, but the question, again, is why did you take it?"

"So you only figured out part of it."

He slapped the arm of his chair. "What are you talking about? What's to figure out? I saw you sneak in here during dinner, and the next day the aluminum bookmark had been replaced with regular old foil. It doesn't make any sense."

"First of all, it wasn't aluminum. But I suspect you realized that. Do you remember what I told you about why I was here?"

"You said you were here to repair distortions in reality."

"More specifically, I was researching the distortion, but I couldn't find the source of it. I spent ages looking for it, but I didn't know what it was—an object, maybe even a person. I could only see its effects. But you're the one who found it."

"That little scrap was the source of your problems? What the hell is it?"

"I don't have that information," she said, and set the foil down gently on the arm of the chair.

"Can you guess?"

"I would say it's a technological artifact, from a device we don't know about."

"Like something from the future that bled through, like we did?"

"Maybe. Or from somewhere else. You've heard stories about alien spacecraft crashing in the desert, correct?"

"Oh, Gilbert loves those. To hear him tell it, the Southwest is like one giant saucer scrap yard. We should get him in here."

She laughed. "It's just one hypothesis, but perhaps something like that happened, and the artifact was overlooked during the cleanup. Subsequently Daniel found it when he was out walking, and then put it in that book in his library."

"So why did you sneak in and take it? Why not just ask Gilbert for it?"

"I'm sure he didn't even know it was there, and he certainly won't miss it. Would you want to explain to him that a little piece of foil was somehow interfering with the structure of reality?"

"No, I wouldn't." He watched her, his fingers caressing the red cotton cover of *The Lost Weekend.*

"But Gilbert is so into you, I'm sure he'd hang on every word you said, no matter how far-fetched the story."

"Yeah, he is, isn't he. I'm going to work on that, now that I have some free time."

"So what are you going to do with it?"

"The artifact? I've already removed it from this area. There are specialists who will study it and try to figure out what it's doing." She looked at him intently. "So how did you manage to activate it? I found it that night because it was glowing white-hot across a whole spectrum of frequencies."

"I didn't do anything to it," he said. He thought for a moment. "I did try to do a psychic reading on it. I held it between my palms to pick up its vibes."

"You must have recharged it."

"Just from the heat of my hands?"

"Maybe. Or maybe it soaked up your psychic energy."

Mason stared at her for a moment.

"You didn't cause any harm, if that's what you're worried about. How did you locate it initially?"

"It was inside this book, and it fell out onto the floor."

"So you just pulled that book off the shelf at random, and happened to find it?"

He thought about it, trying to remember that day. "I put out the vibe that I wanted to find a book related to Daniel's gold brooch, and this is the book that called me over."

"Interesting. Maybe some part of you wanted to help me, even if your conscious mind wasn't party to it."

Mason looked at her but didn't reply. Finally he said, "There's so much going on that I just can't figure out. It feels overwhelming."

"That's just because it's new. Do you know how the air traffic control system works?"

"Oh, god, woman, enough with the analogies."

She held up her hand and said, "Just hear me out. How much do you know about the workings of air traffic control?"

"Nothing, except that it happens."

"And airplane engines—do you know how those work?"

"Not really."

"But you wouldn't hesitate to get on an airplane and fly across the country."

"Not at all, as long as it's summer at the other end."

"Why do you trust it when you don't understand it?"

"Well … I'm confident that other people know what they're doing, and there's sufficient oversight to make it safe."

"So, this is the same. Have some faith that all these things that seem overwhelming and inexplicable are actually working how they're supposed to. You're not going to figure it out overnight, but you're well on your way. I've never seen anyone breeze into a temporal bleed-through the first time as blithely as you did, hocking your jewelry and making friends in the bar."

"Is that what it's called, a temporal bleed-through?"

"You can call it whatever you want."

He nodded. "So is there any advice you can give me?"

"How about this: you're in charge of it."

"You sound like my high school guidance counselor."

"It was true in those circumstances, and it's true now."

"But how do I know what I can manipulate, and what's fixed, and what's just random noise and chance? It's like playing a game where the rules keep changing in every round."

She laughed. "So many questions. But you are the one who has to answer them. Again, you're in charge."

"OK, I get it. No shortcuts," he said, leaning back in the chair. "Another thing. Last night we saw the blue lights over the arroyo. You said that was connected to your distortion issue. If you removed the artifact, why is it still happening?"

"It's a temporal distortion, so it'll be happening fifty years from now, for all I know. The good thing is that by removing the artifact, it won't get any worse."

"I guess that makes as much sense as it's going

to. So what about Hanh—am I going to run into her again?"

"That's up to you, but I'd say you're entwined with her somehow, don't you think?"

"I don't think she likes me very much."

"She helped you out when you needed help. You don't have to like her, but you'll probably run into her again."

"Great," Mason said, not looking forward to it. "What about you—am I going to see you again?"

"That's completely within the realm of possibility."

"That's all I can ask for," he said, grinning. He realized that he trusted Laura now, and enjoyed her company. It was a relief to be around someone who understood.

She leaned forward in the chair. "So I think I've got all the information I need. Have we cleared things up to your satisfaction?"

"Not even close," Mason said, throwing up his hands. "But I suppose it'll have to do."

Laura smiled and stood up. "You'll get there."

She pulled the door open and Mason followed her out into the kitchen. Gilbert was sitting alone at the table, arms folded.

"What's going on?" he said, looking at each of them warily. He was jealous, Mason saw.

"I think we figured out all our psychic business," Laura said. "If you ever need psychic help, Mason is your guy."

"I'm aware of that," he said. "He is pretty sharp."

"And I'm wondering if I could ask for your help today—I have a flat on my car. I have a spare and all the tools, but I could use the help of someone with some muscle."

Gilbert looked about as muscular as a wet ferret, Mason thought, and stifled a grin.

"Oh, yeah, of course," Gilbert said, jumping up. "Let me put on some other clothes, and we can head out."

After he'd gone, Mason said, "Be gentle."

"Don't worry about Gilbert," she said. "He'll be fine. And you—take care of yourself."

"I will," he said, and gave her a brief hug.

After Laura and the positively giddy Gilbert had started walking toward her campsite, Mason found Ned, sitting in Daniel's office working on his computer.

"What time are we heading out?" he asked.

"I was thinking after dinner. We'll give Gilbert one last decent meal before he goes back to microwave burritos. We'll be driving in the dark, but traffic will be light."

"Sounds good. I'm going for a hike. I'll be back in a couple of hours."

"Hold on—what did Laura want to talk to you about?"

"It's a work thing," Mason said, leaning against the door frame. "I'll tell you all about it later."

"Is it paying work?"

"Not exactly, but I'm thinking it'll help with that."

Ned nodded. "Don't get lost out there."

"That's impossible. You can see everything for twenty miles, including this house. The only danger is snakes, and they're all hibernating right now."

"Don't forget about the Sasquatch."

"If I see it, I'll give it your regards," he said.

Mason put on his sneakers and sunglasses and headed out across the desert. He gave Laura's rig a wide berth, walking instead toward the low mountains. There were no distractions here, just nature, which he expected would help him clear his head. It was a lot to process, this new spin on the nature of reality. He had always suspected that there was a lot more going on than met the eye, but he'd never seen it so blatantly in his own experience. Reading jewelry was one thing; walking around in another decade was another thing entirely. But it didn't shake his worldview, he realized, just made it more real, less theoretical. It cemented his career choice as a positive one.

But could he handle having metaphysical experiences that no one would believe? He climbed up on a flat rock that had a view of the valley, and sat there for a while, enjoying the sun and the quiet. He didn't want to lie to Ned about what was happening to him as things got more surreal. But their relationship worked so well in other ways, and despite his skepticism, Ned was easy to be around. No single person can provide everything we need, Mason knew, so maybe he'd have to be content talking about the psychic stuff with Peggy, and sharing other things with Ned, and stop demanding that Ned embrace it.

Maybe it would get less disruptive if he got better at it, as Laura had implied. Maybe the psychic abilities that he was uncovering weren't innovations, either, but rather just an extension of what he'd been doing all along—not new, just new to his conscious mind. He'd definitely have to integrate his burgeoning skills with the other parts of his life.

LATER ON, BACK AT the house, Ned made comfort food for Gilbert, mac and vegan cheese and a carrot and cashew meatloaf. The mood at dinner was light, with Gilbert animatedly regaling them with the story of his heroic assistance to Laura, helping her change her flat. She must have orchestrated that somehow, Mason thought. Watching him talk, Mason realized he really had come to like Gilbert, despite his blind spots. He was a straightforward guy, and he didn't mean any harm. Peggy laughed loudly at Gilbert's story; she seemed lighter, happy to have recorded at least one decent song, and relieved at having started the process of getting to know her brother.

It was well after dark when they loaded their bags into the trunk of the Crown Vic, along with Peggy's guitar case and the empty cooler. Peggy clambered into the backseat, and Ned drove, as always.

Gilbert waved good-bye, calling, "I'm going to starve without you, Nedly."

"So he finally got a date with his desert-rat muse," Peggy said as they started off along the dusty road. "I hope she doesn't trample his heart."

"He'll be fine," Ned said. "That reminds me—Mason, what was your secret meeting with her all about?"

"Well, it's complicated," he said, completely truthfully. "Basically she's had some psychic experiences like mine, and she wanted to encourage me to develop my own abilities."

"Seriously? I never would have thought that about her," he said.

A set of headlights appeared in the distance, and Ned and the oncoming car dimmed their lights simultaneously.

"I wonder who that is," Ned said. "Gilbert didn't say he was expecting anyone."

"I know exactly who that is. It's us," Mason said. "Watch. It's a Crown Vic, same color as yours because it *is* yours. Take a look at who's driving."

He glanced at Mason, a concerned look on his face. "Did you get sunstroke out there this afternoon?"

"Wait for it," Mason said.

Ned navigated the car close to the right side, but the road was wide enough that he didn't need to slow down. Sure enough, the Crown Vic rolled past them, and Mason caught a glimpse of Ned in the driver's seat, staring straight ahead, and Peggy in the shadows behind him. He felt the hair rise on the back of his neck. He was relieved that it was too dark to see himself on the far side of the car; that would have been too much.

"What the hell?" Peggy said, shock in her voice.

"What did I tell you? That was us."

"Not possible," Ned said softly, staring straight ahead.

"How could that be us?" she asked, leaning over the front seat. "I mean, it looked like us, but we're right here. What the hell is going on?"

"It's called a temporal distortion. It's related to the blue lights we saw. Do you remember driving up here on Friday? We had the same experience in the opposite direction."

"I don't remember that."

"You must have blocked it out, the way Ned is doing right now." He poked Ned's shoulder.

Ned didn't look away from the road. "We're almost at the highway," he said dreamily.

"Who's the space cadet now?" Mason said.

"That doesn't make any sense," Peggy said.

"Even Gilbert was aware that weird stuff happened up here, remember? It's a whole bubble of odd phenomena."

"I guess it's good that we're leaving, then. The blue lights were plenty odd for me—I don't need to be seeing copies of myself running around."

She poked Ned's shoulder as well.

"What?" he said, irritated, but didn't look at her.

"His brain just can't handle it," Mason said. "He'll snap out of it when we're away from here." Ned's reaction made him think he was right not to tell him the whole truth.

"It's freaking weird. Mason, how can you handle all this?"

"I just take it as it comes," he said.

Epilogue

A COUPLE OF WEEKS LATER, on Wednesday, Mason was eating breakfast in the kitchen, the noonday sun streaming in the French doors. Ned walked in from the office, and without a word pushed Mason's coffee cup aside and set his tablet in front of him.

"What's this?"

"Something you should see," Ned said. "Just press 'play.'"

It was a news item from a local TV station. "Museum officials are confident that their 1978 compensation payment effectively means the pin is the museum's property," the voiceover was saying, but more compelling was the video—the camera zoomed in on Gilbert's swirly, flowery brooch, delicately cradled in a pair of white-gloved hands, the flicker of flash photography glinting off the magnificent piece. The camera pulled back to show a room of beaming bureaucrats facing a crowd of journalists jostling for a better view. The video cut to a mustached man whose thick neck bulged over his tight shirt collar. The banner at the bottom of the screen read "Lt. Walsh, LAPD Art Crimes Division." Over the staccato clicking of camera shutters, he said, "We're very happy to get the royal pin back, but it's important to remember that there is no statute of limitations on certain kinds of art crimes. We'll be investigating this case extensively, and we encourage anyone with any information to contact the art crimes division."

Mason paused the video. "That makes me really happy. Gilbert's given it back to the world. I think I have a crush on him now."

"Don't tell him that, or he'll want to move in."

"I had no idea that the LAPD had a whole division to investigate art crimes. That's concerning."

"That investigation stuff is all lip service. They'll never connect it to Gilbert. He probably shipped it to them anonymously, with the help of one of his conspiracy buddies."

"I'm not worried about him. If they get wind of that second song Peggy played us, though, she could go away for a very long time."

———•———